UNABLE TO BREATHE, I STOPPED THE CAR COMPLETELY.

Then the wave of nausea hit. I put the car into park and bolted out the door, diving to my hands and knees, dry heaving. Nothing came out, but my stomach didn't care.

"Try to relax, Theodora. You're fighting it." I felt a strong, soothing hand on my back.

Mack might as well have been stroking my breasts or inner thighs or kissing my lips. His touch felt intimate, tender and sensual.

Okay. Feeling better now. In fact, I felt the urge to jump to my feet and kiss him like a long-lost lover I missed with all my heart.

I shook my head from side to side, gathering up my crumbling wits. *Oh look. I'm in the doggy position on the ground with my tongue hanging out. Nice.*

I wiped my mouth with the back of my hand, and Mack gripped my arm to help me to my feet.

This is it, I realized. I was going to turn around and look him straight in the eyes. I already knew how beautiful he was, but the last time we'd locked eyes, it changed me.

Copyright © 2015 by Mimi Jean Pamfiloff

All rights reserved. No part of this publication may be reproduced, distributed, or transmitted in any form or by any means, including photocopying, recording, or other electronic or mechanical methods, without the prior written permission of the writer, except in the case of brief quotations embodied in critical reviews and certain other noncommercial uses permitted by copyright law.

This is a work of fiction. Names, characters, places, brands, media, and incidents are either the product of the author's imagination or are used fictitiously. The author acknowledges the trademarked status and trademark owners of various products referenced in this work of fiction, which have been used without permission. The publication/use of these trademarks are not authorized, associated with, or sponsored by the trademark owners.

ISBN-10:0996250484
ISBN-13:978-0-9962504-8-1

Cover Design by EarthlyCharms.com

Editing by Latoya Smith and Pauline Nolet

Interior design by WriteIntoPrint.com

OTHER WORKS BY MIMI JEAN PAMFILOFF

COMING SOON:

TOMMASO

(Standalone/Paranormal/Humor/Immortal Matchmakers Series, Book 2)

GOD OF WINE
(Standalone/Paranormal/Humor/Immortal Matchmakers Series, Book 3)

TAILORED FOR TROUBLE (Standalone/Romantic Comedy/The Happy Pants Series)

IT'S A FUGLY LIFE (Standalone/Contemporary Romance/Fugly Series, Book 2)

THE TEN CLUB (Standalone/Dark Fantasy/The King Series, Book 5)

BRUTUS (Standalone/Paranormal/Humor/Immortal Matchmakers Series, Book 4)

READ NOW:

FUGLY (Standalone/Contemporary Romance)

IMMORTAL MATCHMAKERS, Inc.
(Standalone/Paranormal/Humor/Book1)

FATE BOOK (Standalone/New Adult Suspense/Humor)

FATE BOOK TWO (Standalone/New Adult Suspense/Humor)

THE HAPPY PANTS CAFÉ
(Standalone/Prequel/Romantic Comedy)

THE MERMEN TRILOGY (Dark Fantasy)

Mermen (Book 1)

MerMadmen (Book 2)

MerCiless (Book 3)

THE KING TRILOGY (Dark Fantasy)

King's (Book 1)

King for a Day (Book 2)

King of Me (Book 3)

THE ACCIDENTALLY YOURS SERIES
(Paranormal Romance/Humor)

Accidentally in Love with…a God? (Book 1)

Accidentally Married to…a Vampire? (Book 2)

Sun God Seeks…Surrogate? (Book 3)

Accidentally…Evil? (a Novella) (Book 3.5)

Vampires Need Not…Apply? (Book 4)

Accidentally…Cimil? (a Novella) (Book 4.5)

Accidentally…Over? (Series Finale) (Book 5)

To: Silvia

MACK

The King Series

Book Four

I hope you enjoy the crazy ride!!

Mimi

Mimi Jean Pamfiloff

a Mimi Boutique Novel

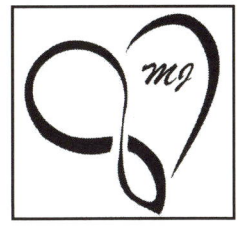

Like "Free" Pirated Books?
Then Ask Yourself This Question:
WHO ARE THESE PEOPLE I'M HELPING?

What sort of person or organization would put up a website that uses stolen work (or encourages its users to share stolen work) in order to make money for themselves, either through website traffic or direct sales? **Haven't you ever wondered?**

Putting up thousands of pirated books onto a website or creating those anonymous ebook file sharing sites takes time and resources. Quite a lot, actually.

So who are these people? Do you think they're decent, ethical people with good intentions? Why do they set up camp anonymously in countries where they can't easily be touched? And the money they make from advertising every time you go to their website, or through selling stolen work, **what are they using it for? The answer is you don't know.** They could be terrorists, organized criminals, or just greedy bastards. But one thing we DO know is that **THEY ARE CRIMINALS** who don't care about you, your family, or me and mine. **And their intentions can't be good.**

And every time you illegally share or download a book, YOU ARE HELPING these people. Meanwhile, people like me, who work to support a family and children, are left wondering why anyone would condone this.

So please, please ask yourself who YOU are HELPING when you support ebook piracy and then ask yourself who you are HURTING.

And for those who legally purchased / borrowed / obtained my work from a reputable retailer (not sure, just ask me!) muchas thank yous! You rock.

The unauthorized reproduction or distribution of a copyrighted work is illegal. Criminal copyright infringement, including infringement without monetary gain, is investigated by the FBI and is punishable by fines and federal imprisonment.

DEDICATION

To Anson and Marleen, my desert spirit guides.

"Anson! Look! It's soooo beautiful!"

MACK

Prologue

MACK

Most know me as Mack, though I have gone by many names and have lived many lives—each ending in misfortune. Each making my heart grow colder and harder.

This is my story—a tragedy without hope, so don't try. Don't wish for an ending filled with love or a moral lesson that lifts your soul. That's impossible for a man like me, because I have done too many terrible things.

So turn back now if that's what you're looking for. Run the other way.

The only ending you should expect is mine. And I pray that this time my death is an irrevocable one.

Chapter One

TEDDI

"You've nailed it," I mumbled to myself, eyeing my black pencil skirt and pinstriped blazer in the mirror, confident that no one would ever learn my little secret.

Or would they?

I swiveled in my black heels one last time before realizing I was running late for my first day.

Yep. A new job.

Thus the reason for my new look—dark brown hair cut into an A-line and extra-thick, black-framed glasses (instead of contacts) to play down my green eyes.

Of course, just because I looked more grown-up and serious didn't mean the staff would accept a twenty-eight-year-old woman named Teddi (short for Theodora) as the new director of the Santa Barbara Mental Health Treatment Center. I could hardly accept it myself.

However, my youthful appearance only held the

number two slot on my list of concerns. Coveted number one was the sort of obstacle a conservative suit could never resolve. I only hoped that no one caught on.

No one has yet, I thought to myself. Really, only my parents knew the truth.

Whoa. Don't get me wrong. I wasn't some breed of degenerate. I was what most considered lucky—a child prodigy who skipped several grades, graduated high school just shy of sixteen, and finished my PhD in clinical psychology from Colombia at twenty-two, which included taking a year off from my studies to try to find myself.

A disastrous failure.

Because for every ounce of academic intelligence I possessed, my emotional intelligence decreased by an equal amount. Yes, my brain was broken. So in laymen's terms, I *got* everything and I *got* nothing. A computer had more genuine empathy, yet I could probably build one from a blueprint if I had to.

So what was wrong with me?

Who the hell knew? But the doctors explained it as this: the deep emotional part of my brain was shut off.

That wasn't to say I didn't have emotions. I had some, although nothing anyone would classify as normal. A normal person, for example, would feel happy when her boyfriend of two years proposed. I'd felt…indifferent. Just like I felt when I caught him four weeks later pounding his dick into my best friend while I was supposed to be at work. While he wore my lingerie. My brand-new, untouched wedding-night lingerie.

The appropriate response would've been outrage; however, the best I could muster was the conclusion that fate had intervened at an opportune moment and done me a favor.

So, as you might guess, this lack of emotion was what drew me to psychology—the study of the mind and emotions. And it was why I owned a collection of Spock T-shirts.

Yes. I really did. And that was as close as you came to humor when you've spent your whole life trying to understand why you're broken.

Anyway, now you see why it was a miracle that I was given the opportunity to run a center. Because while my analytical mind could pinpoint schizophrenia or bipolar disorder from a mile away, and I immediately knew the most effective treatment for every patient I met—it was my gift—I found it difficult to connect to people. But that didn't mean I couldn't be useful in this world. I just went about helping people in a logical way.

Watch out, Spock. Here comes Teddi.

"See you later, Bentley." I turned and patted my dog's head—a Jack Russell with a serious staring problem—and then grabbed my keys to my new black BMW (a little congrats gift to myself) before heading out the front door of my two-bedroom beach house.

This is it, Ted. Don't fucking blow it.

೧೪

My new administrative assistant, Shannon—a middle-aged blonde with a passive-aggressive smile—greeted me at the center's reception. The one-story glass building, with excessively vibrant landscaped grounds, was a mere ten minutes from downtown Santa Barbara and contained two hundred beds, fifty of which were reserved for long-term care. The rest were for the weekend benders, meltdown moms, and variety of people simply going through an anxiety rough patch. Substance abusers and alcoholics went to the rehab center across town.

"And here is our resident patient ward," Shannon said, gesturing toward the set of beige double doors with small windows to prevent the staff from slamming into one another. "Fifty patients who receive around-the-clock care, including one-on-one and daily group therapy."

Shannon pushed through the doors, and I followed along, feeling a bit like I was being led on a tour of a people zoo.

"These first ten rooms are for our suicide watches. The others are a variety of conditions—PTSD, chronic postpartum, eating disorders. The usual." Shannon strolled along the hallway, waving her hands toward the different doors as she spoke.

There was nothing here I hadn't seen during my last four years working at County, which meant most of these patients were textbook. Roughly seventy percent would respond to standard psychotherapy treatments. The other thirty percent were statistically likely to require life-long care, show little to no improvement, or require a treatment we weren't able to provide.

My job was to ensure the center ran efficiently and benefited as many patients as possible.

"And that's the tour!" Shannon said cheerfully, her brown eyes reflecting a different emotion altogether, while we stood at the end of the hallway.

Suddenly, my gaze was pulled down the immaculately polished, beige tile floor, gravitating toward the last room on the right. The small frosted-glass window was completely dark.

"Who's in that room?" Room twenty-five.

"Which room, Dr. Valentine?"

A hard shiver sprinted through my body, and I rubbed my goose-bump-covered arms. "It's a little cold in here, isn't it?" Yes, we wanted to watch our expenses, but this was a little much.

Shannon shrugged. "I feel okay."

Hmm. "I'll look into the thermostat later." I then pointed at room twenty-five. "And that? The room with no light inside despite it being ten in the morning and our facility having a strict rule about keeping to a schedule." Routines were important for everyone—sane or not. So was sunlight. And no, the room couldn't be empty. Not possible given we were full and turning people away from our lovely sanctuary of mental healing.

"Oh. That room…" Her eyes shifted a bit. "That's Dr. Wilson's patient."

"Does the patient have an aversion to light?" Because obviously the curtains were drawn inside and the lights were off.

"Not that I'm aware of."

"So then?" I asked.

"Well, that patient is a little..." She leaned in to whisper, "He's difficult."

"I'm not following." After all, that was our purpose: dealing with difficult people or people with difficulties.

She drew a breath so deep that her sagging posture almost looked correct for a moment. Almost. "He won't speak to anyone, so Dr. Wilson gave us instructions to leave him alone until he's ready."

I lifted my chin and pushed my glasses back up my nose. "If the patient isn't willing to engage in his own healing process, then we can't help. Send him home or transfer him to County." This facility was private, but operated mainly on grants from the state or donations, so we had a mandate in our charter to process a certain number of patients each year.

Shannon blinked at me.

"Are you confused?" I wasn't sure what her blinking meant—not so obvious to someone like me.

"Dr. Wilson was very clear; the patient is not to be disturbed."

Ah! Meaning, Shannon didn't want to upset Dr. Wilson. "I see, Shannon. My apologies. It wasn't my intention to put you in the middle." This was a classic example of how my brain worked. The human-feelings element was generally an afterthought. I did try my best, however, to be aware of such things. I truly did. It was why I'd adopted a dog to help cultivate my ability to pick up on subtle emotional cues. So far, Bentley only stared a lot, as if waiting for me to do something.

I continued, "I'll ask Dr. Wilson myself about Mr. Room Twenty-Five later. No action required on your part." I offered Shannon a smile, hoping she'd know I meant no harm. *I'm just a robot soul in a people suit. Don't be frightened, human.*

As we concluded the tour and walked away, I couldn't help looking over my shoulder at that little dark window. Why was it so fascinating to me?

I shook it off, and Shannon then showed me back to my office—a bland-looking rectangle with a wall of windows facing the parking lot. Suited me fine. I wasn't into fancy feng shui. Or mood lighting. Or anything that wasn't functional. Desk, two chairs, computer, bookcase, done.

We discussed the schedule for the week, including staff meetings and patient progress reports. For someone like me, it was all very logical and simple. I still was unsure, however, how the staff and doctors twice my age would respond to my…well, youthful appearance.

After Shannon took her leave, I sat at my desk, staring at a pile of paperwork, wishing I could feel more excited. This was a big accomplishment, something to be proud of—my parents certainly were. And my best friends, Melody and Sue, were certainly impressed. But like every milestone in my life, I felt little more than like I was checking off boxes while waiting for my real life to commence.

This is your life, Ted. Stop wishing it to be something else.

I grabbed a piece of paper and a pen and started making my action plan for the week. I found lists to be soothing. But only just a little.

#1. Review doctor/patient load

#2. Have Shannon set up one-on-one meetings with staff

#3. Review cash flow with accountant

And…oh!

#4. Talk to Dr. Wilson about Mr. Room Twenty-Five…

Chapter Two

I spent the rest of my first week checking off my list: reviewing the books with Martha, the head accountant; planning my first staff meeting; and scheduling those one-on-ones with the other doctors—schedules were extremely tight, so Shannon was doing her best to clear space. I noted immediately how understaffed we were, and that meant doctors had too many patients. I'd have to cut costs—bye-bye resort-style meditation gardens—and hire additional doctors. Turning away more patients was not an option.

So in the meantime, I would take on a few patients of my own. It was very unorthodox, but it would show the troops I was willing to roll up my sleeves.

Interestingly enough, Dr. Wilson had twice as many patients as anyone else, which was why I had Shannon put me on his calendar late Friday afternoon.

"Dr. Valentine! Come in. Come in!"

I entered Dr. Wilson's untidy office and introduced myself, thinking how he reminded me of my father. He had thinning gray hair, a round belly underneath his white coat, and large brown eyes. I liked him immediately.

"So," I said, taking a seat in the black pleather chair facing his desk, "I've spent the week evaluating workloads and noticed you have more than your fair share of patients."

He sat back down behind his desk—a cluttered mess of files and sports knickknacks. "Yes, well, I tend to get many of the patients the other doctors don't want."

"That is not acceptable. We don't get to pick and choose who we help."

"Not all of the doctors feel they're equipped to handle every case," he replied.

They all had general degrees in psychology—same as me. Okay, not the same as me. I had three specialties: neuropsychology, cognitive and neurolinguistics psychology, and psychometric and quantitative psychology. Basically, I was a thoroughbred psycho. (That would be me using my humor there. You see…psycho is short for psychologist, which insinuates that—oh, neverthehellmind.)

"I will correct this immediately," I said. "In the meantime, I plan to handle a few of your cases. Simply let me know which ones you recommend I take." I wouldn't want to undermine any current treatments.

Dr. Wilson puckered his wrinkly lips in

contemplation. Behind him sat a wall of medical books that hadn't been touched in years—probably since the day he started working here. The inch of dust had to be a health code violation, but I would let it slide. Because I was a wild woman. (See. There's my humor again. I wasn't wild at all and—oh, forget it.)

"That's very kind of you, Dr. Valentine. I'll think it over and give you a list on Monday or Tuesday."

"Great. Oh, and before I forget, I wanted to ask about the patient in room twenty-five."

Dr. Wilson sipped from his chipped "#1 Dad" mug on his desk. It was probably filled with vodka. The man had to be under a considerable amount of pressure and seemed suspiciously happy. (That wasn't a joke, in case you were wondering.)

"Ah, you mean our infamous Mr. John Doe," he said, setting down his mug.

"But we're a voluntary treatment facility. John Does—" i.e., people who suffered from amnesia or refused to give an identity "—go to County."

Dr. Wilson smiled. "Yes, he checked himself in a week ago. Paid for three months of treatments and then asked to be put in a room and left alone until he was ready to talk."

"That's insane," I said flatly.

Dr. Wilson laughed with a husky voice that reminded me of a rent-a-Santa. Ho, ho, ho… "Why, yes. I suppose it is. And what better place for him than here."

"So the man doesn't want to be treated, and we

have no idea why he's here?"

"Not a clue. But isn't it interesting?" Dr. Wilson seemed genuinely excited by this very inefficient use of our facility's space. I couldn't understand why.

"He can't stay. There are people who require our assistance and are being turned away."

"He did pay for the space," Dr. Wilson pointed out.

"It's not a matter of money; it's our obligation to help the community. But there's a nice five-star hotel down the street that will gladly accept his money and offer him solitude."

Dr. Wilson nodded. "Yes, well, I do see your point."

I stood, extending my hand. "Good, then. It's been very pleasurable speaking with you, Dr. Wilson."

He rose from his seat, reaching out to shake my hand. "I look forward to working with you, Dr. Valentine."

I thought that the interaction had gone extremely well; however, when I got to the door, Dr. Wilson threw at me, "I hope you don't mind addressing the matter directly with our John Doe? The rest of my day is very full."

I offered a cordial nod. "Of course, I'll see to it immediately." Not as though I cared about hurting John Doe's feelings. We had a job to do here.

And, to be quite honest, I was now curious to meet this Mr. Room Twenty-Five.

❧

Darkness was the one thing in this world I didn't care for—probably because I felt most comfortable with facts. Seeing objects equated seeing facts. *There is the floor. There is the couch.* Facts.

Guessing where things were—*I think the leg of this table is around here somewhere—ouch!*—was inefficient, useless. It was why night-lights were invented.

So when I entered John Doe's dark room, the first thing I wanted was to bring in some light.

"Mr. Doe?" I said to the dark figure seated in the corner of the small room, staring at me like an eerie scarecrow waiting to frighten the shit out of anything that crossed its path. "My name is Dr. Valentine. I'm the new director. May I turn on the lights so we can discuss the reason you are here?"

"I asked not to be disturbed." The man's deep, masculine voice felt like a cold, chilling slap. Yet strangely, it was also…Well, I didn't know, really. Hypnotic, perhaps.

I squinted, my eyes straining to see his face but only able to make out his silhouette—broad shoulders, short hair, and fit-looking arms from the shadows of biceps I was able to spot. I could also see he wore dark pants—likely jeans—and a white tee shirt.

"That's exactly why we need to talk," I said. "It's come to my attention that you are not here to seek therapy—"

"Leave."

My mouth flapped for a moment. "I'm sorry, but you—"

"I said *leave*," he growled.

Sadly for him, intimidation didn't work on me. Not that I was stupid and wouldn't get out of harm's way. The question was, did he intend to harm me?

"And if I don't?" I asked, testing the waters. His response would tell me everything I needed to know.

I waited for a reply.

And then I waited some more.

He's not going to answer me. Fine. This was silly and a completely unproductive use of my time. I would just have to see him with my own two eyes. My gift would do the rest.

"Okay. These lights are going—" I flipped the switch, and the moment my eyes met his, I was hit by a hard wave of…

"Holy fuck," I gasped.

I flipped off the lights, turned, and left the room. *Fuck. Fuck. Fuck. What was that?*

Chapter Three

That was not real, Ted. That was not real, I repeated to myself, fleeing back to my office through the brightly lit corridors, panting the entire way. I rushed past Shannon, who was trying to get my attention about some meeting, before I slammed my door shut.

Holy shit. I held my hand over my heart. The muscle pumped at a vigorous pace, a direct result of my body's fight-or-flight response.

I leaned forward, planting my hands on my knees, catching my breath. *Super. I'm having a nervous breakdown on my first week of work*. That was the only explanation for what I'd just seen.

But *what* had I seen?

Oh, God. Those eyes. They were a vivid blue, like something straight from a Monet. And his face was so…

Crap. I couldn't recall what he looked like. I only remembered what he felt like: Rage. Pain. Hate. Thirst. Danger. I felt them all, right down to the marrow of my quaking bones.

I blew out a breath and put myself upright, my head spinning with a potent elixir of sensations and emotions. Yes. Emotions. Goddamned emotions!

There was a light knock at my door, and I quickly smoothed down my bob and brushed my hand over my puckering white blouse to flatten it.

"Yes?" I said calmly, trying to hide the tremor in my voice.

Shannon's blonde head peeked through the door. "Dr. Valentine, sorry to disturb you, but I have those reports."

All I could see was her passive-aggressive smile. And this time, I felt irritated by it.

Holy shit. I care?

"Sorry?" I had no clue whatthehell she was talking about. All I could see were those eyes. *So blue. So…beautiful.*

"The reports," she clarified. "The ones you wanted before I left for the weekend."

Oh. Those. "Thank you, Shannon."

"Are you all right?" she asked, handing me a folder. "Your face is red."

I touched my cheek. I was, in fact, flushed, and I was pretty damned sure that tickle in the small of my back was nervous beads of sweat.

"I'm fine," I said. "Just a little overworked this week. That's all."

"Well, I think you did great—you catch on quickly. Especially for someone so young."

I wasn't certain if she meant it. She may have simply been probing for my age.

"Thank you." I gave her a polite nod and went to pack my things for the day, feigning calmness. Home would be a more suitable place to digest the event. Whoever that man was, something about him was…wrong. So very, very wrong.

No. That makes no sense. Don't project this onto him. Logic would say that the event was in my head—triggered by something external, something indirectly related to him. For all I knew, an ordinary apple could've evoked the same response. An apple or a breeze or something random that my mind inadvertently connected with.

But deep inside my gut, this didn't feel random at all. And neither did my instant obsession with Mr. Room Twenty-Five.

༄༅

That evening I took Bentley for a long powerwalk on the beach, ignoring the fact it was mid-February and unusually cold outside. Normally, I wouldn't risk lowering my body temperature and getting sick. And normally, I would've gotten irritated with the way Bentley stared, as if to say, "Hey, lady, you suck at being a dog owner," but tonight my mind was filled with other worries. At least, that was what I guessed the knot in my stomach and heaviness in my heart meant.

What happened to me today? I thought while stretching on my wood-framed balcony overlooking a not-so-pacific view of the Pacific, the roaring waves rippling with moonlight. *My brain feels like that ocean.* Rolling and thundering with an invisible, unstoppable force all its own. A door had been kicked open inside me. *But why would flipping on the lights and locking eyes with that man do this?*

Once again, an image of those vivid cobalt blue orbs played in my head, but I still couldn't remember his face.

Whatever this was, I wouldn't be solving it tonight. Perhaps in the morning I might resort to calling my father. He was a retired psychologist, now living in Scottsdale, Arizona, with my mother to pursue a life of cactus gardening, golf, and sunshine.

No. You don't require help. You're still Ted Valentine. You're in control. Capable. You can deal with this.

Of course, those were all just empty words because I had zero explanation for what was happening.

Thinking that a well-rested mind might help, I went to bed early. That night I dreamed of running down a steep dirt hill, the sun burning my back while I was chased by a man with a gleaming silver sword, his face covered in blood. When I was unable to run any further, I looked down at my muddy burlap dress. I was already bleeding from a deep wound. I then looked up at the approaching man, and all I could see were two stunning blue eyes framed by a face covered in deep crimson.

Then it all faded away.

※

The next morning I craved sausage. Sausage and eggs and cheese. I felt ravenous—like a person who hadn't eaten in weeks.

I shuffled through my freezer, wondering why all of my food was so healthy and bland. Frozen chicken, peas, and some plain spaghetti Lean Cuisines. Inside my refrigerator were bags of prepared salad, bottled water, turkey, and bread. No mayo, dressings, hot sauces, or anything fatty or spicy.

"Who *is* this person?" I said under my breath, running my hands over the top of my head and catching a glimpse of Bentley sitting there staring at me judgmentally.

"For fuck's sake! What are you looking at? Haven't you ever seen a person go crazy?"

He continued staring as if to say, "No. You're my first, you crazy bitch."

"Yeah, well…fuck you back, Bentley!"

He practically rolled his eyes at me and headed for the little grassy side yard through his doggy door, seeking better company outside. Tree. Squirrel. Hermit crab. Whatever.

I went back into my depressingly sterile-looking bedroom—white comforter, white armchair, reading lamp, a white dresser, and a clock—slipped on my jeans and a tee and grabbed my car keys, heading straight for the drive-thru. I purchased two breakfast croissanwiches and a mocha with extra whipped cream and chocolate syrup. I inhaled everything, noticing how each bite of the salty fat tasted like an orgasm in my mouth, born from some dark delicious world and better than any sex. Yes, I'd had sex. And I'd had orgasms, too. They were pleasant when I was lucky enough to achieve one, but I'd never understood why so many people obsessed over getting off. I much preferred a good jog or a hot bath. Those were beneficial to my health. But this morning, my taste buds felt like they were connected to every part of my body. I'd even caught myself moaning at a stoplight while I chewed a piece of gooey melted cheese.

Crap. What's happening to me? The cheese wasn't even real.

I found myself heading for the center, desperately needing to see Mr. Room Twenty-Five one more time.

༄

My black BMW came to a screeching halt in my parking space. I turned off the engine, jumped out, and rushed inside, doing a crazy-speed walk toward the residents' wing. Somewhere inside the mental chaos, I heard the weekend staff greeting me as I walked the long corridor, but I could only focus on one thing: him.

When I got to his door and stared at the small rectangular window absent of light, a cold shiver swept through my body.

Ohmygod. I couldn't believe it, but I felt genuinely frightened.

Doesn't matter. I need to see him. I twisted the handle and pushed. My breath immediately caught as I spotted my mystery man sitting in the corner, facing the doorway as if expecting me.

"Hello," I said, my voice full of pathetic and unfamiliar quivers. "Do you remember me from yesterday?"

He didn't reply, nor did that seductively muscular silhouette flinch an inch.

"I'm going to assu-u-umme that you do," I stuttered, pushing a lock of my hair behind my ear. "This will sound crazy—and the fact that a psychologist is saying that is humorous, I get that—but I need to know who you are."

"Why?" he said in a jarringly deep voice that filled the room.

I stepped back but stopped myself from running out the door as I had yesterday. Instead, I focused on his question. I wanted to tell him the truth. I wanted to share with someone what had happened to me. And somewhere in the back of my discombobulated head, I believed him to be the only person on the planet who might comprehend. Nevertheless, telling a patient that they've triggered a possible psychotic break in their doctor wasn't wise. (A) It would not instill confidence. (B) It might make them feel guilt over something they truly weren't responsible for. (C) They were not here to help me; it was the other way around.

I straightened my back. "Well, I ru-run this facility, and it's my job to know who we're treating. I have to ensure you're getting the right help." I balled my hands into tight fists, hoping he wouldn't notice them shaking.

A long moment passed, and I watched the shadows of his menacingly thick arms rise up as he laced his fingers behind his head and leaned back in the chair.

I was getting the impression that this man wasn't sick and that something else was going on.

Either way, he hadn't answered my question. Either way, I needed to know. Either way, it felt like my life depended on the answer.

"Who the *hell* are you?" I asked again, my voice filled with false bravado.

A stiff-drink-worthy moment passed, and I felt his blue, blue eyes burning into me, though I couldn't see them.

"My name is Mack."

Chapter Four

Mack. His name was Mack. But the way he'd said it, it could've been Satan or Dark Angel or the name of some mythological creature born from temptation where one's sinful fantasies were fulfilled.

"Mack," I repeated, drinking it in.

"Yes. And you should leave here before it's too late."

"What's going to happen to me?" I asked, trying my best to sound serious versus condescending and skeptical. These new emotions were like crazy little fuckers shooting off firecrackers in my head.

"You might die."

Okay. Not encouraging. "Meaning, you intend to kill me?" I tried moving toward the emergency call-button to the side of the door—every room had one—but the novel sensation of a hot messy panic had my feet stuck to the floor.

Another long, tense moment passed, and I felt genuinely torn between jumping right into treating this disturbed man and helping myself. Of course, I wasn't sure how to do either. Not enough information. And then there were all of the things going on inside my body. Every frantic heartbeat, every shallow breath made me feel alive for the first time. The only way to describe it was like that scene in the *Wizard of Oz*. Black and white shifting to Technicolor. So even if I wanted to walk away, I couldn't. The brilliant colors were what had always been missing from my life.

"I would never harm you. Intentionally, anyway. But the threat I refer to is my curse," he said, with a bleak seriousness that had me believing him for one sad mental-moment. However, this man was delusional. Plain and simple.

"So this curse will cause you to kill me," I concluded.

"Let's just say that it makes me a hazard."

"So then why are you here?" I asked, probing for any possible insights into his mind. "Why not just run off and live in the mountains so you don't risk hurting anyone?"

"Because I've come here to die," he stated coldly.

All right. I had not been expecting that answer. Of course, logic would say there were a million other places to die.

My conclusion?

The man knew he was not well and wanted to live. He wanted help. There was simply no other reason for him to be here.

As for me, the effect this man had—unlocking some corner of my mind that allowed me to feel intense emotion—had no explanation. But I needed to separate the two. Whatever was going on with me didn't concern him.

"Then I would like to help you break this curse, Mack," I said to placate him. "I would like to help you live."

"I cannot be helped."

"I know you might feel that way, but I'm the only one truly qualified to make that determination."

He laughed. "You should leave now. You don't know what you're getting yourself into."

"I know you've come here because—"

"Make no mistake, Dr. Valentine, I am here to die. In peace. And hopefully soon before they find me."

"*They* who?"

He did not reply.

I let out a breath, thinking this over. I needed him to start talking. I needed to see the world through his eyes so I could fix him.

"In that case, you can stay for as long as you like," I lied. Everyone had to leave eventually. "However, there's a price."

"I already paid." He sounded displeased, but not the sort of way a normal guy might. There was a bite of menace in his voice. I couldn't let that get to me.

"Not good enough. But I'll make you a deal; if you tell me more about your curse, you can stay."

"Just as long as I *chat* with you," he said, sounding amused.

"Yes. I want to hear how it happened."

"You will not believe it."

"Thinking for me, are you?" I replied.

He was silent, so I hoped that meant he was mulling over my proposal, but I wanted to see his face and know for sure. I reached for the lights.

"I wouldn't do that if I were you," he warned.

I pulled back my hand, remembering what happened the last time. But that had all been in my head. Right?

"Okay," I said. "We'll leave the lights off for the time being. Do we have a deal?"

"It is your life. But are you so certain you're willing to risk it for simply hearing my story?"

Ah yes. Because he believed I would die if I spent time with him.

"We'll begin on Monday." I turned to leave, attempting one last time to get a look at his face. A shadow, a hint, a something.

Nada.

"I look forward to it." He dipped his head, and a sliver of light peeked through the curtains, catching the side of his face. The stubble-covered jaw was strong and angular. His cheekbones were chiseled works of man-art.

My heart raced and my mind—without any warning—filled with hot, hard, simmering sensations that felt like an erotic drug. That, of course, was where I had to put my mental foot down. Chaotic situation or not, there were some lines that should never be crossed, like murder, hitting children, or kicking puppies. Having sexual feelings for a patient was also on that list somewhere.

"I look forward to it, too, Mack." I left, eager for the light outside that felt like my personal sanctuary, a place where I could breathe again. But as soon as I got into the hallway, the need to go back into that room and bathe myself in that delicious darkness called Mack overwhelmed me.

For Christ's sake, get a hold of yourself, Ted.

Chapter Five

Once I got home and calmed my jittery nerves (with the aid of a greasy jalapeño cheeseburger and fries, due to still feeling like I had years of culinary deprivation to make up for), I thought the worst was over. With some comforting junk food in my belly, I would begin the process of dissecting the events and identifying the catalyst for my new mental state.

But as I sat on my balcony, bundled in a warm purple sweater and scarf, my mind simply wouldn't settle. I thought about calling Sue, one of my best friends (who hadn't slept with my ex), but she was at some librarian convention in Minnesota. I tried Melody, my other best friend, also a non-backstabbing-whore to the best of my knowledge—but it went into her voicemail. I didn't leave a message, of course. What could I possibly say? "Hi. It's the new me. Crazy, hungry, and with real emotions versus the fake ones you've come to know and love over the years." Best to tackle all that another day.

I leaned back in my red Adirondack chair and felt the cold night wind picking up. I suddenly felt a dark heaviness in the air, like a cosmic storm brewing just for me. Was it a sign of things to come? Probably. I was already chomping at the bit to get back into that room again and listen to the sound of that hypnotically deep voice, feeling my toes clench and my pulse accelerate.

I craved it. Yes, more than fake cheese.

As soon as I arrived at the center Monday morning, I asked Shannon to block out my entire day. I would lie to myself and say it was best to give Mack as much time as he needed to talk.

"Are you sure?" Shannon asked, sitting behind her immaculately organized desk right outside my office. "Because you have Doctors Cole and Snow scheduled back-to-back for their one-on-ones."

"I'm sure. I have to see a patient of Dr. Wilson's."

Shannon gave me one of her passive-aggressive smiles. She didn't like my request, and this time I was quick to pick up on her emotion: Irritation.

This is what I've been missing? The world was so much easier to navigate when you understood what people were subtly saying with their eyes or body language.

"I know you worked hard to schedule everything, Shannon. I'm so sorry. But the patient really needs someone to listen to him. I don't think anyone ever has."

Shannon's eyes softened a bit.

Sympathy. That's sympathy! I mentally patted myself on the back.

"You're right, Dr. V, he probably needs you more than the other doctors do."

"Thank you for understanding, Shannon. And…Dr. V?" I lifted a brow.

She shrugged. "Your last name is kinda long. Hope you don't mind."

"Dr. V" made me think of Dr. Vagina or Dr. Viagra or Dr. Vaseline or…

Why am I thinking about that?

"Let's stick to Valentine." It sounded more appropriate and, frankly, it had always helped soften my cardboard-like image.

"Okay," she said with a quick shrug. "Good luck with John Doe."

I was about to tell her his name, but I found myself wanting to keep it to myself, like some strange coveted gem that belonged only to me.

Damn, next I'll be sitting in a swamp, wearing a ratty thong and petting a ring.

"Thanks." I grabbed my notebook and headed straight for my delicious cosmic storm, not bothering to batten down the hatches. I wanted to feel every drop of stinging rain, every gust of wind, and hear every bolt of deafening thunder. I'd never been more excited in my life for anything.

Or anyone.

I knew I wasn't the only person in contact with Mack at the center. After all, the man was brought three meals a day and the janitorial staff cleaned his room—trash, clean sheets, and towels, etc. But when I approached his door and heard a soft voice on the other side, it instantly struck me as…well, it made me cranky, frankly.

He's mine.

I mentally jerked back from my reaction, pressing my hands to my mouth. *Holy shit. What was that?* I had never felt possessive of anyone. Not once.

I shook it off and reached for the door, but as I did, it opened and out walked a short and extremely thin blonde woman in very tight red pants.

She stopped inches from my face with a gasp, almost plowing into me.

"Who are you?" I asked. She wasn't staff, and she had no visitor's badge.

She looked me over as if I were a piece of gum stuck to the bottom of her zebra-striped heels. She then stepped around me and started walking away without so much as a word.

"Excuse me, but I asked you a question." As I spoke, the strangest, vilest sort of hatred began bubbling out of me. Yes, I hated the woman. And it wasn't because she'd just dismissed me.

"Keep on going, then, sweetheart…" I growled, wanting to rip her teased blonde hair from the roots, while I watched her disappear out of sight down the hall.

Whoa. This is too much. I gathered myself with a

few quick breaths and then turned the handle and stepped inside the dark twelve-by-twelve room. The institutional beige curtains were pulled shut, and the bathroom door to the side of the room, opposite the twin bed, was closed tight, creating a cave-like feel.

As expected, Mack's menacing frame sat in the corner. He was so still that he could easily be mistaken for a statue.

"Who was that?" I asked.

"A friend. And before you ask which sort, I'll save you the trouble—I used to fuck her. Now I don't. She does favors for me, hoping I might change that."

The word "fuck" instantly triggered nude images of Mack sliding between my thighs, his firm bare ass pumping hard, his back flexing with powerful muscles, making every inch of my body burn with ecstasy.

I swallowed down a nonexistent glob in my throat. "Good to know," I said, masking my involuntary response. "So I take it she's not one of these people you're hiding from." Mack had mentioned that "they" were looking for him.

"No."

I waited for more, but he wasn't giving. And for the time being, I needed to pick and choose my battles. The priority was helping Mack realize why he was really here: He wanted and needed help.

"So are you ready to begin our session?" I asked.

"Actually, I've changed my mind."

What? "Meaning?"

"Exactly what you think it means."

"But you—"

"A moment of weakness," he said, cutting me off. "I see no point in mulling over my situation with a stranger."

Dammit. Why did it have to be so dark in here? He really needed to see the annoyance in my eyes.

"Then why did you say you agreed to my terms?" I asked.

"Because I thought I might like to seduce you. One last fuck with an attractive woman before I go." I watched the dark shadows of his shoulders shrug. "Who can blame me? You look like you're in need of a thorough fucking. And it's been a while for me."

I couldn't even begin to respond to his shocking statement, but the space between my legs knew what to do: Agree with him. Not that he was the one to end my sexual drought. The man was not right in the head. And he was my patient.

"I see you're silent on the matter," he said. "So I'll take that as a confirmation."

I shook my head at him. "Whatever you're doing won't work," I said flatly. "I've met far worse than you."

"Really?" He leaned forward a little in his chair. "Do tell."

I normally wouldn't discuss other patients, but I needed him to open up. So that meant I had to make the first offering. "I once treated a man awaiting trial for murder. He made Hannibal look like a kitten."

Mack chuckled. "So he tried to eat your liver?"

"No. He said he would hunt down my mother, rape her, and then eat *her* liver. He kindly offered to videotape the event and supply me with a copy."

That had happened over a year ago, and of course, I hadn't been one for panicking or reacting, so that had just made the insane man angrier. Yes, he had been restrained for our sessions.

"And this man," Mack said, his tone full of cockiness as if he didn't believe me, "what became of him?"

"After three sessions, he was IDed by the police as a suspect in another murder case. He's now serving a life sentence."

"What was his crime?"

I folded my arms over my chest. "Raping his ex-girlfriend's mother and then killing her. He was apparently unhappy about getting dumped. He thought that was a good way to get that across to his ex."

Mack was no longer chuckling. "So this man, you say, didn't frighten you and, therefore, I do not frighten you."

"Are you planning to eat any of my body parts?" I asked.

He paused for one moment too many, giving my brain the opportunity to make up an inappropriate, sexually explicit response related to which body parts I might enjoying him "eating."

Jeez. Focus, Ted. Focus.

"I am not a fan of liver," he finally replied.

I shrugged. "Then there you go." I took a seat at the small table pushed against the wall, not too far from the door, and set down my notebook, folding my hands in my lap. "I'm a very good listener, Mack."

"And I said I'm not interested in talking." His tone was firm, and his masculine voice sent a ripple of shivers over my skin. I knew I wasn't supposed to enjoy it, but I did. I felt so alive, like I was sitting in the lion's den, all my senses on high alert.

Then, nothing happened. *Fine. Hardball it is.*

"All right. I understand." I got to my feet and turned toward the door. "I'll have your discharge papers ready within the hour."

"I'm not leaving," he declared calmly.

"We had a deal—you broke it. So I say you *are* leaving, and I have two large orderlies who will agree with me. And if you try to hurt anyone, your next stop will be jail or the county psych ward, where you'll be sedated—because, sorry, we don't prescribe meds here. We're all about talking." The part about sending him away was all a lie, of course. I wouldn't send him anywhere. Not in a million years. Whoever this man was, I felt a gnawing need to keep him.

I resisted the urge to laugh at myself. I wasn't afraid of being in a dark room with a man who declared I would die from some sort of curse contagion. I was afraid of never seeing him again.

"You play a mean game of ultimatums, woman," he said with a hint of a smile in his baritone voice.

I reached for the door handle. "I'm fair. And I believe in keeping my word. Welshers don't win any points with me."

"A man is allowed to change his mind."

I smiled. "Then change it."

"You realize that once we begin, there's no turning back."

My stomach turned into flutters of excitement. "I understand."

"And you understand that you cannot save me. That's not what this is about."

Oh, but I c*ould* save him. And I could help myself in the meantime. "I understand."

"Then sit, Dr. Valentine. And get comfortable."

"Please, call me Ted."

"Ted? This is a man's name," he said, sounding displeased.

No. Really? "Teddi, then, if you prefer."

"Teddi sounds like something soft and furry. You are anything but."

Gee. Thanks. "Theodora, then."

"Theodora." My name rolled off his tongue like a seductive potion, sending sensual chills through my body.

No, Ted. You're getting confused. So many new emotions mixed inside my head, but I needed to remember that he was still the patient. There was no sensual anything here. Me. Him. Therapy.

I retook my seat and folded my hands. "Whenever you're ready."

Chapter Six

MACK

Calm the hell down, man, I told myself, attempting to settle my unstable mind.

Wasn't easy.

Being near Theodora felt like having my body drawn and quartered, each appendage bound to a different emotion that threatened to tear me to pieces. Despair for what and who I was. Anger because I was unable to control it. Fear that I might repeat history. Again.

Yet somewhere, buried deep inside, was a flicker of hope that my torment would soon end. I merely needed to persuade Theodora to make it happen. That was what this was all about, this game I was playing to carefully lure her in.

I drew a steady breath and decided the best place to start was at the beginning. I would need to ease her toward the truth. Her own mind would do the rest and nudge her into the light.

If for some reason that didn't work, well…I

could always torture her to get what I wanted.

Yeah, I think I might like that. She looked like she needed a good whipping.

Fuck, Mack. I pulled myself back from the dark ledge. I had to remember who I really was. Or used to be: someone who wasn't an angel, but had a few redeeming qualities.

I cleared my throat. "My real name is Callias Macarias Minos, the second son of Archon and Elysia. And brother to Draco, my twin who was born a few minutes ahead—more than enough to set my life on a different path from his—or so I thought." In reality, we'd ended up on very similar paths.

Theodora uncrossed her legs and straightened her back. Every movement of her curvy body amped my salacious urges. And then there was her voice and sweet smell. Even the way she wore her dark hair cropped right at her jawline, calling attention to her delicate neck, was pure temptation.

"You—you have a twin?" she asked.

Yeah. Get the fuck over it. He's taken. Of course, once her memories began returning, she'd remember what a ruthless bastard my brother was.

"I do," I replied. "And while my brother would become leader one day, I would be groomed to serve him. At least, that was the hope of my parents. However, after they passed from an illness brought over from the mainland via one of the local merchants, I decided to abandon any pretenses of becoming my brother's obedient servant."

"So," she interrupted, "you lived on an island. Where exactly?"

"In Greece." Or, more accurately, what would one day become Crete. But I would get to that part in a moment.

"I see. So it sounds like you didn't like your brother much," Theodora said, keeping her tone neutral. I assumed she wanted to keep up with pretenses of her own and tell herself this was a clinical evaluation of sorts. It wasn't, of course. Somewhere deep in her soul, she knew our meeting wasn't a coincidence. She knew that something terrible would happen once I reached the end of my story. This was her fate. And mine.

"I loved my brother," I replied. "But I felt my time was better spent fucking and drinking. After all, I was free from any real responsibility. Why not enjoy it?"

"How'd that work out for you?"

The ugly answer sat right in front of her with a heart so cold and a rage so deep, I could barely breathe some days. Unless those were the days I killed someone. Killing was the only thing that gave me relief. Temporarily.

She looks like she'd give me another type of relief. I could practically smell her arousal in the air.

No, Mack, I censured myself. *You are not going to touch her.* Still, I already felt a war beginning to rage inside me, and the clock was ticking. My not-so-kind side always triumphed.

I continued, "My life was great until my bastard

of a brother came to me one day with a request—a favor—which I did out of guilt."

"So, you did this *favor* for your brother. Then what?" She shifted in her chair. I knew she felt anxious sitting in the dark, but looking at her face would only make things more difficult for me. The less I saw of her, the better. At least, that had been my plan going in. Now, I wasn't so sure it would make one hell of a goddamned difference.

Still, I had to push forward. I had to make her see the truth.

"What happened next wasn't pretty," I replied to her question. "More like the beginning of a long nightmare. However, Draco never asked for anything. Not once. The bastard was too proud for that. Which is why I couldn't turn my back on him."

"What did he ask you to do?"

"He asked me to fight him to the death—his death," I replied.

I could see the frame of her body going still.

"And you killed him," she concluded correctly.

"Yes. Draco had executed a woman named Hagne, who attempted to murder the love of his life. Unfortunately, Hagne's death, even if justified by our laws, was a problem. She was what we called a Seer, a sort of sacred priestess, if you will. Her family was very influential and threatened civil war if they didn't get Draco's head, something I would later learn was inevitable—the war part, I mean."

I could not see the expression on Theodora's face, but I did not need to in order to infer what she was thinking: This man is insane.

Sure the hell am. But not the way you think, sweetheart.

She leaned back a little in her chair. "So you gave them his 'head,' but it didn't save your people." There was blatant skepticism in her voice.

"Do you find my story difficult to believe?" I asked.

"Frankly, it sounds like an old gladiator or Viking movie. Tales of betrayal and fights to the death."

Vikings? Those assholes? "I assure you, none of what I tell you is fantasy. And for the record, Vikings weren't nearly as impressive as on TV." They were more like overgrown sewer rats with big swords.

She glossed over my comment and asked, "How did you feel after your brother—what was his name again?"

She was testing to see if my mind was working correctly.

"Draco." Later, he would be known in Athens as Draco the Law Giver, the man who birthed the very first written law in ancient Greece. He was also a cruel motherfucker, thus the term Draconian. Of course, today he went by the name King. Just King—the man was a powerful narcissistic asshole, through and through. And how was he still alive? I would also get to that part in a little while when the moment was right.

"Ah, yes. Draco," she said. "So how did you feel after you murdered your own brother?"

"How do you think I felt?"

"I'm not you, so you'll have to tell me." Her glib tone was beginning to poke tiny holes in the wall I'd built to keep her safe—for the moment—from the darkness inside me.

"Are you certain you want to hear this part?" I questioned.

"You've asked me this several times. Why would I say I want to listen to you if I didn't? I have plenty of other patients to see."

"So I should be grateful?"

"No. You should answer my question," she snapped back.

God, how I wanted to stand up, march across the room, and spank the hell out of her. Then I would take her mouth with mine and remind her why she should always be respectful and obedient in my presence. Then, I would bend her over and fuck the hell out of her.

Goddammit. I gripped the arms of the chair, digging my nails into the wood. This situation was going to be more difficult than I'd thought.

"Perhaps we should continue another day," I said, keeping my voice low and steady while my heart pounded in my chest, my dick getting rock hard as my brain produced images of her bare ass and breasts.

No. I can't do this again. I can't be with her. Everything I needed depended on keeping my distance. It was for both our sakes.

"Mack, we made a deal. If you don't want to continue, then don't. But then you have to leave."

I knew that was bullshit. She wanted me to stay.

She wanted to see where this would go. Fate was like a drug that had drawn us together.

"I'm waiting, Mack," she prodded. "Continue with the story or leave."

I cleared my throat, allowing Theodora to think she had some sort of control over this fucking mess so she'd stay calm. At least for another ten minutes.

"I ended up being taken by a very unfriendly tribe of Nords. They made me a slave, which nearly killed me." This was the part of my story I'd never told anyone. It seemed pointless to share the misery. Especially with Mia, who would only blame herself for what was to become of me. King would only know what he stole from my head—bits and pieces of memories I'd shoved away in a dark corner of my mind.

"Mack? Exactly how old do you think you are?"

I was wondering when you'd ask that, sweetheart.

༺❦༻

TEDDI

"Have you ever heard of the Minoans?" Mack asked with a dead-serious tone, that deep delicious voice bouncing off the sterile walls.

I uncrossed my legs and thought it over for a moment. I'd been out of school for a very long time, but I had an excellent memory. "Ancient Crete. Pre-Christ. I don't remember much else."

Please, don't tell me you think you're over three

thousand years old. Because that would make him even crazier than I'd thought.

"You know more than most," he said, seeming pleased.

Yeah, well, I could've graduated high school at fourteen if I'd wanted, but I convinced my parents to let me stay one more year. Not that I'd been afraid—impossible for me—but I had been debating on career paths—a coin toss between anthropology and psychology. I would've double majored, but the best programs were at different universities.

"I should know more," I said, "but it's been a while since I cracked open a history book. But let's get back to—"

"You wouldn't find much on the Minoans. They disappeared after I beheaded their beloved king and was forced to flee the island. Civil war devastated them, and any survivors were overrun by mainlanders."

Oh no. This was what I was afraid of. "So you're saying you're…?"

"I was born in 1430 B.C. Give or take a few decades."

Cough, cough. Did the guy think he was a vampire? I had one of those once—obsessed with the Twilight series. He'd even insisted everyone call him Edward and wore plastic teeth. Now that I thought about it, it was goddamned funny.

"You do realize how old this would make you?" I said.

"Over three thousand years."

He had to be testing me. Because Mack seemed

far too rational and lucid to believe such a fantasy.

That or he's psychotic. Something I hadn't ruled out.

"You wouldn't mind if I turned on the lights, would you?" I asked. "I've never seen a three-thousand-year-old man."

"You're mocking me."

"No." I shook my head, realizing that I actually was. My emotions were out of control. "I mean, yes. I'm sorry. That wasn't very professional, but I'm not feeling myself lately."

"I can relate."

"So you're over three thousand years old. Obviously this far exceeds the lifespan of a normal human being, so I assume there's a reason you've managed to defy nature."

"There is," he replied, a curtness in his voice. "But I haven't gotten to that part of the story yet."

"Okay, then. Please continue."

"If you don't believe my age, I assure you that you won't believe the rest of my story."

He had a point, and I had the impression this man was very skilled at reading people. Patronizing him in any way wasn't a wise choice.

"Then convince me," I said candidly. "I've got all the time in the world."

He laughed. "If only you understood how true that actually is."

Chapter Seven

MACK

1395 B.C.

Where the hell are we going? I thought as I sat chained to the wet wooden rowing bench of the small sailing vessel, my stomach so empty I could feel my body turning on itself, consuming my muscle tissue and less important organs to keep me alive.

Waste of time. I was definitely going to die.

No longer able to feel my raw, bleeding hands, I stopped rowing—something that would normally earn my back several lashes from the bastards who held me and fifteen other men captive. Tonight, however, there would be no lashes. Only death.

It was pitch black out, the stars and moon masked by the storm clouds that rained havoc on the rickety boat. A boat that was no longer seaworthy and filling with water.

I glanced over my shoulder, barely able to make

out the silhouettes of the four men with buckets, frantically battling the invading saltwater flowing over the edge of the ship.

Yes, a complete waste of time. Didn't these poor bastards realize that the gods did not wish us to live? We'd been at sea for well over a month, our captors in search of new lands to plunder, I assumed. But those men were greedy fools. The drinking water was gone. The food stores were nonexistent. What little fish we caught wasn't enough to sustain so many men. But every time I entertained giving up, I remembered what I carried.

I placed my bloody, numb hand over the leather pouch around my neck. Inside was what looked like a plain rock—which was the reason my captors allowed me to keep it. The rock, however, was the key to bringing back my dead twin brother. The one I beheaded upon his request, something I regretted with all my heart.

I closed my eyes and said a silent prayer to the gods. *If this is my last night on earth, I beg of you to see that this stone is returned to Mia. Please, it is all I ask.*

I never did learn how the stone worked, but I knew that the love of my brother's life, Mia, was a Seer with powerful gifts. Before my brother died by my hand, she had bound his soul to this earth so he could not leave it, using the rock so that one day they could find each other again. How? I did not know. I only knew that I had taken the stone by accident when I'd been forced to leave Minoa—ironically, Mia's doing. She did not want me to die at the hands of our people, who rioted over the loss of my brother. So she used her gifts to force my guards—men from a particular bloodline who'd guarded our kings for centuries—to take me away. But within days of leaving, I discovered the rock hidden inside a basket used to carry my valuables. I fought the guards tooth and nail to return to Minoa, but they were under Mia's commands, unable to do anything but obey her orders to take me far from the island. They were killed by the men who were now my captors.

I laughed like a madman under my breath. *You gods must truly despise me*, I thought, the rain pelting my raw, sun-chapped face.

The man to my side, a farmer from the mainland, who once had the muscles and strength of an ox but now resembled a skeleton, slid his hand to my shoulder. At first, I expected him to spew yet another ridiculous lecture about hope, but I quickly realized he was simply trying to hold on to anything he could.

Our ship capsized.

The gods truly do hate me. But why?

༄༅

My first thought when I came to was that I was dead. However, the dead didn't feel their faces and bare chests burning from the hot sun, their ribs didn't throb with multiple cracks, and their lungs didn't spew saltwater and blood.

But the beautiful topless woman with long black

hair, large brown eyes, and creamy dark skin, kneeling over me, had to be sent from the heavens. I'd never seen such a lovely creature.

"Finally," I mumbled, "the gods are doing something kind for me."

The woman spoke in a strange tongue, her voice filled with sweetness as she lovingly stroked my face with her soft hand, as if trying to comfort me.

But the moment I heard strange male voices screaming off in the distance, I questioned my assumption about being dead. So then where the hell was I?

Within seconds, a group of extremely short men with deep dark skin and strange black symbols painted over their bodies showed up and began poking me with sticks.

"Leave me be," I said. I now know I must've looked like someone from a faraway planet. With my height—considerably tall, even by my people's standards—light blue eyes and a black beard that matched my hair, I was probably the first Caucasian they'd ever seen. They kept jabbing at me to see if I would bite. Of course, I was far too weak for that. And before I knew it, they were dragging me through the jungle.

When I woke again, lying in a roughly woven hammock, half out of my mind with pain, thirst, and hunger, I was in a small mud hut with a fire pit in the middle. The same lovely woman kneeled over me, lifting my head to drink.

I sipped only a little before the taste had me retching.

"What in the gods' name is that?" I muttered.

She simply smiled and then swabbed my forehead with a damp cloth that smelled like sweet fragrant herbs. I assumed she believed speaking was a waste of effort since we couldn't understand each other. In reality, I picked up new languages quickly, but I felt much too tired to do much of anything besides lie there and hope to die quickly. The pain was intense despite her presence soothing my soul. She exuded a quiet, loving energy I instantly connected with.

Did she feel the same? I wondered.

My eyes took in the small dwelling adorned with strange animal hides stretched out on wooden frames, along with dozens of sticks that were tied together to form symbols.

Talismans, I realized. Our Seers used similar trinkets to communicate with the spirit world.

I looked back at her and noticed the way her eyes stared without fear or question. Like she knew something I did not.

She's a Seer, I realized. *Dear gods, that's what she is.* I assumed they weren't called that by her people, but it didn't matter. The gods decided which bloodlines were gifted with powers. They decided who was chosen to carry out their will.

"*Uk'ik*," the woman mumbled and then reached for a small wooden bowl. She wanted me to drink again.

"No, no, thank you," I protested. "I think I'd rather die."

"*Uk'ik!*" Her brown little nostrils flared.

"You don't like being told no, do you?" I said.

She pointed to the bowl and then my mouth, smiling stubbornly.

"I suppose whatever it is, it's not poison." I lifted my head obediently and caught a glimpse of her beautiful creamy brown breasts and dark nipples. The women of my island went topless much of the time, so breasts weren't much more to me than a neck or set of lips; however, something about this woman's body captivated me. Even on my deathbed, I wanted to touch her. Every silky inch.

She helped raise my head a bit higher and seemed pleased when I drank the concoction. She then pushed me back and stroked my cheek.

"That made you happy, didn't it?" I said.

She stared for a moment. "Hap—py?"

"Happy." I gave her a weak smile, the best I could do.

"Happy." With a grin, she stood and gestured for me to stay and then left the hut. I imagined she went to be with her people somewhere not too far away.

So who was she? And where the hell was I? I didn't know, but I felt as though the gods had guided me to this place to die peacefully. Only, now I felt a tiny spark of desire to live. Something about this woman made my soul flicker with light.

༒

Over the next few weeks, I saw the woman—no one else—twice a day. When she was gone, I missed her company, especially the exquisite view. When she came to stoke the fire and bring fresh water and food—some strange mush mixed with meat—animal unknown—she would stare at me the way women do when they want a man. Yes, I was no stranger to women. Taking my pleasure from them was one of my favorite pastimes back on my island. Drinking wine had been the other. It was why my people had loved my brother and not me. He cared for them, helped them, and protected them. I did none of those. Draco and I were similar only in our looks—blue eyes, black hair—identical, in fact, but that was where our similarities ended.

As for my host in this strange new land, I tried to learn her name, but it was useless. She would only gaze at me with those soulful brown eyes. Such temptation. But frankly, as much as I wanted to stay and continue trying to communicate, I had to face facts: I was becoming stronger, thanks to her gift of healing, which meant I had to attempt to return to Minoa. My redemption was counting on it, as was the soul of my brother, whose tortured spirit now wandered aimlessly between this world and the heavens. Unless I returned the stone to Mia, my brother would remain that way for eternity. I couldn't allow that. *As long as it takes, whatever I must do, I will bring my brother back and return all that I robbed him of.* Yes, I'd killed him because he'd demanded it. But I should've said no. I should've told him to fight Hagne's family and that I would've stood by him in battle. But no, like a fool, the fool I'd always been, I'd let my brother do the thinking for me.

On the eve of the twentieth day, my beautiful companion sat next to me on a little stool beside the hammock I lay on.

She held out a bowl of food, offering it with her usual smile.

"No food," I said, gently pushing her hand away. "I need a boat."

She looked at me quizzically.

"Boat," I repeated and rose from the hammock. She took the opportunity to steal a glimpse at my manhood as the small cloth tied around my waist slipped off.

I won't lie, she looked pleased, and my ego felt the same.

I resecured the cloth and plucked a small twig from the ground, drawing a boat in the dirt. Around it, I drew little waves and the symbol of a fish.

When she realized what I meant, I could see the disappointment in her eyes.

"Boat," she repeated the word.

I nodded. "Yes, boat. I need to go home." I drew another symbol on the floor of an island with a house. Inside, I drew little figures of people. "Home."

A look of deep turmoil reflected in her eyes. More than ever I wished I could explain how grateful I felt for her help, how special she was to me. She'd saved my life and asked for nothing in return.

When she stood, I assumed she was going to go speak with her elders in the village, but she did not leave.

She untied the colorful piece of woven cloth around her waist and dropped it onto the floor.

With a hard breath, I took in the sight of her soft curves and the patch of dark hair between her legs, knowing that I shouldn't dare touch her. I knew nothing about these people or their customs.

But when she slid her hands underneath the piece of cloth I wore around my own waist and began stroking my cock just aching to burrow deep inside her, my manly needs took over.

I reached for the back of her head and kissed her soft lips with a roughness I didn't know I'd be capable of in my still-weakened state. But this kiss, like the woman, was nothing ordinary. As I tasted her on my tongue and pulled her sweet scent into my lungs, something deep inside me burst, like a light flooding my entire soul and blocking out the entire world. There was only her and me, and nothing else seemed to matter.

Where had she been all my life? Because she was the meaning I'd been searching for without ever knowing it. And I believed she felt the same for me.

Our gentle kiss quickly turned into a wild flurry of touching—our bodies grinding, our hands exploring.

Dear gods, could her breasts be any softer? Every part of her I touched—ass, hips, and the soft folds between her legs—was sinful perfection.

She broke away and began to kneel, clearly intent on getting my cock into her mouth, something I would normally not refuse from a woman. But that was not at all what I wanted. I needed to be inside her, to feel our bodies connected.

I gently grabbed her shoulders to raise her up. "A woman like you should never kneel before a man like me." I knew she did not understand the words, but I hoped she'd sense how I truly felt.

I guided her into the hammock and then laid myself between her thighs, not wasting a moment's time to position my cock at her entrance, testing her readiness.

Gods, was she ready—warm and wet with eager hips.

With our mouths once again locked in a flurry of frantic kisses, I thrust myself into her and she let out a yelp. I immediately realized why. *Virgin?*

"I am sorry," I said, pulling back. The thought hadn't crossed my mind. She wasn't young. In fact, I guessed she might be five or six years older than myself. On my island, a woman of her age had already had two or three lovers and several children.

Staring deeply into my eyes, she slid her soft hands around my ass and urged me back.

"I don't want to hurt you." I hoped she might understand. My size wasn't something a woman would enjoy her first time.

She gave me a tender smile, as if to tell me it was what she truly wanted. And me, being who I was, could not resist the invitation. I sank into her, slowly driving in my cock, inch by inch. She moaned gently into my ear, tilting her hips to help me slide deeper.

She pulled her head back and stared at me with those intense eyes, and I wondered what she was thinking. What did she see in a man like me who had washed up on the shore, his body shattered and emaciated, nearly dead?

I didn't know the answer to that question. All I knew was how she made me feel, like there was a goodness inside me—something worth wanting.

Slowly, we began moving together, our eyes locked, our souls touching. It was like magic the way our spirits and bodies mingled and drew from each other. My heart began to tingle, as if pulling the light from within her. Meanwhile, I felt her pulling a piece of my soul into her.

There were no words to explain other than she was pure ecstasy, pure light, pure sinful pleasure and joy.

With what felt like only seconds of thrusting and sliding my shaft into her willing but tight body, I felt the eruption coming. I quickened my pace, our hips colliding, her pants coaxing me to take more, to move faster, to drive harder. I exploded inside her, feeling my seed pouring over the tip of my cock, bathing the entrance to her womb while she dug her soft fingertips into my ass, pushing me as deeply as I could go. She let out a cry of ecstasy, and I forced myself to continue, drawing the pleasure from her body.

Finally, after several long moments of lying together joined, sweaty, and spent, I opened my eyes to find it was no longer morning, but nighttime. What seemed like minutes had really been an entire day.

I looked at her and stroked her soft cheek. "Who are you?" I whispered.

"Happy," she responded.

Happy. That was the perfect name for my Seer from another land. She made me so happy.

☙❧

The next morning, I found myself alone as usual, but now I missed her more than ever. Her sweet smell, her eyes, her smile. I realized that being with this strange woman was the first time I'd ever felt I belonged somewhere, like there was hope for me. Yet, the other part of my soul knew that to be impossible. I was an outsider, not welcome in their village.

"Boat," I heard a familiar voice speak from the doorway.

I looked up and found my goddess holding out several spotted furs and three big bundles tied with twine.

"Boat," she repeated, urging me to take the goods.

"You did it?"

I got up, and she quickly shoved the items at me. "*Ko'oten. Ko'oten!*"

I suddenly had the feeling she was telling me to hurry my ass up. Whatever was going on, it wasn't with the blessing of her tribe.

"You will get in trouble," I said. Of course, she didn't understand. Her response was to grab my hand and urge me to follow.

"No. I do not want you to do this." I had no clue if these people were peaceful or savages, if her helping me to take a boat would earn her more than simply being poked with sticks as they had done to me when I invaded their shore.

I dug in hard and with my considerable size compared to hers, she couldn't move me. "No," I said firmly. I refused to have another black mark on my soul or cost someone else theirs.

Suddenly, deep male voices began echoing through the jungle.

Her eyes filled with panic. "*Ko'oten!*" she yelled.

"I will speak with them. I will tell them you had nothing to do with this."

Frustrated by my lack of movement, she shook her head at me and blew out a breath. She then reached for my hand and placed it over her heart. "Happy." She laced her fingers with mine, and I then started to wonder if she was trying to say that she wanted to go with me.

I could never allow that. There was little chance of any boat crossing back over that ocean. I couldn't put her in danger.

I took her hand and placed it over my heart. "You have to stay here."

She blinked at me and then growled, jerking her hand away. She turned her petite frame and began running.

"Gods be damned, woman! Where are you going?" I chased after her, running as fast as I was able, ducking under branches and thick vines. Still fairly weak and not yet having built my muscle back, I moved as fast as a pregnant ox at best.

I tracked her footsteps through the moist dirt, finally breaking through the vegetation, shooting out onto a warm beach covered with white powdery sand. I caught sight of her running toward a small fishing boat that was narrow with an upward-pointing tip.

She didn't stop until she got to it, and when she did, she immediately began shoving off, motioning for me to come.

I looked up at the sky for a moment, trying to collect my thoughts. I had to make her understand.

I hurried toward her, and the moment I got to the boat, now bobbing in the shallow waves with her wading knee deep beside it, I heard the men's voices.

I looked over my shoulder at them as they came rushing toward us with long spears in their hands.

Curses of the gods. This was not good.

Happy yelled frantically, and I had to choose. She would most likely die if we shoved off and tried to cross that ocean. If she stayed, I might be able to bargain with these people and convince them this was my doing. Perhaps I could make them think that I had bewitched her in some way.

I grabbed the boat and gazed into her eyes. "I'm sorry. I can't take you on that ocean. I care too much for you."

She frowned at me and a look of hurt showed in her eyes. She didn't understand, and there was no way to explain it.

The men surrounded us, and that was when I knew that I had once again made a mistake.

CHAPTER EIGHT

TEDDI

Why did he stop? Why the hell. *Did. He. Stop?* I realized I'd scooted forward, literally sitting on the edge of my seat, hanging on every word in that dark room. Yes, it was a fictional story—obviously—but as he wove his tale, using that deep, hypnotic voice, I had been transported to another time and place. I saw every detail he spoke of plus many more he hadn't—the earthy smells of the jungle, the thick texture of the air, the sunlight filtering through the tree canopy—as if I were right there with him. My heart was even pounding and my palms were sweating. I felt torn for the two of them. And the sex—dear God, had he been trying to torture me? It took everything I had not to drool on my lap. No, he hadn't gone into too much detail, but it wasn't necessary. Like I said, my mind felt plugged in to his memories, and anything he didn't say, my imagination filled in.

You're an idiot, Teddi. The story's not even real.

Just like that cheese you ate yesterday. Regardless, my heart genuinely ached for this couple.

I cleared my throat and settled back in my chair, trying to gather myself. "S-so what happened next?" I asked, sounding only slightly less desperate than I felt.

It took him a while to respond. "Are you sure you're ready to hear this?"

"I'm asking, aren't I?"

"You're a bit of a smart mouth."

I was really more of a person who lacked experience in the couth and diplomacy department. One needed to be finely attuned to the feelings of others in order to excel in those particular areas. But that was neither here nor there, and I wasn't about to talk about my issue.

"Yes. And don't change subjects," I reprimanded.

He rose from his chair, and the action startled me. His place was over there on the other side of the room. My place was over here close to the exit.

I was about to get up and head for the door, but then he walked over to the window away from me.

"I'm not changing the subject," he said, his voice quiet and pensive. "I'm merely being a gentleman and warning you—the rest of the story is not a pleasant one." He cracked open the curtain and gazed outside at the plum tree in the courtyard, shattering the intimate cocoon of our little world and bathing the institutional white walls and marbled tile floor with bright light.

Begrudgingly, my eyes adjusted, and once they

did, I sucked in a quiet, appreciative breath. *Dear God*. The light filtered around him like a seductive aura, giving me my first breathtaking glimpse of his masculine, godlike silhouette and the back of his tall—six three or so—body. His shoulders were powerhouse broad and tapered down into a tight waist. His legs, incased in dark jeans, were muscular and long. His hair was dirty blond and a bit shaggy in the back, just enough length to run one's fingers through while fucking like two sex-starved animals with only hours to live.

Wow. Why the hell had I thought that? The "two hours to live" part, I mean. The part about animals was obvious. The man was huge. Or, maybe huge wasn't the right word. He was more like impressive, the sort of guy who walked into a room and drew everyone's eye—the men because they'd see him as a threat. The women because they'd be wondering if he looked just as good naked as he did clothed.

As I ogled and he stared out the window, he lifted one arm against the glass and rested his forehead for a moment. That was when I noticed his heavily inked biceps with what look like dates and symbols and such.

"What do the tattoos mean?" I asked.

"I thought you wanted to know what happens next in my story."

"Can't I ask about both?"

"You can ask," he replied, his tone indicating that he wouldn't necessarily answer.

Pill. This man is a pill. Yeah, but he's a sexy pill, so there is that in his favor.

"I choose story," I said. "Your body art can wait for another day."

I watched his large, powerful shoulders rise and fall a bit with an anguished sigh. He then snapped the curtains shut, pulling us back into his world of darkness. But now, more than ever, I ached to see his face. Did his front look just as good as his backside?

He turned and took his seat while I sat there like an eager puppy waiting for my next treat.

"Well?" I said. "What happened?"

"What do you *think* happened?"

Ugh. He's toying with me. "I don't know, Mack. That's why I'm asking."

I heard a grumble of displeasure from across the room. But then finally, he gave me what I wanted.

"They separated us. I was brought back to that small hut on the outskirts of their village, where I was guarded by several men. She was taken elsewhere. I spent the next several weeks begging to see her and trying to explain that she'd done nothing wrong, but they seemed more interested in me. They spoke to me and asked questions. We traded words, and I learned anything I could, treating it like a game. I would walk my fingers across my palm, pretend to drop dead on the floor, or hold something in my hands, and they would shout out words, like a sad game of pre-Hispanic charades. With my knowledge of languages, I picked up the basics quickly."

"How many languages did you speak?" I asked.

"Sixteen."

That was a heck of a lot of languages. "I thought you said you were from a small island."

"Our people were known for our metalwork and pottery. We traded with merchants from as far away as Eastern China. I really spoke closer to twenty languages if you want to include dialects from nearby fishing villages."

"Impressive."

"Not really. My father insisted I learn so that I could better serve my brother someday—translation skills, math, reading and writing. And, of course, fighting. Everything was planned around my brother's needs."

Except that Mack had said he blew all that off after his parents died. It was why he'd felt too guilty to say no when Draco asked Mack to kill him.

"So you learned Happy's language," I said.

"Enough to communicate and learn her name was really Óolal."

He pronounced it Oh-a-lahl. A beautiful name—sounded like some kind of decadent dessert.

He went on, "And I learned enough to ask them to see her. Instead, I got a visit from Kan, Óolal's father."

"I'm guessing he wasn't happy?"

"He wasn't the sort of man you'd want to cross. And considering my crime, I was shocked that I wasn't tortured to death, my organs plucked out on an altar to appease the gods for my misdeeds."

"Just for taking a boat?"

"No. Turned out, they didn't care about the boat. Kan was their king, and Óolal was considered sacred because of her gifts. She was thought to be the property of the gods. I apparently defiled that gift."

Oh shit. Now I was beginning to understand why this story wasn't going to end in a happy place. No pun intended. "So you took something that wasn't yours."

"Kan and I developed a strange but close friendship over the next several months while they waited for the equinox—the day to make sacrifices and atone for one's sins in their culture. Kan asked questions about the places and people I'd seen while traveling with the Nords. He shared details about his powerful bloodline and his gifts. And every day, I asked to see Óolal but was told it wasn't time yet."

My skin began to crawl as I envisioned where this was heading.

"Ironically, I caught some sort of illness. My guess: Malaria from the mosquitos. I didn't live long enough to find out what would've happened on the equinox, but on my deathbed, Kan promised to bury me with the Artifact—that stone I carried—and mark the grave. I hoped someday someone would find it and that the gods would do the rest, making sure the stone made it back to Mia."

"That was very generous of Kan."

"I threatened to bring his people bad luck if he didn't help my spirit rest soundly."

"Did you ever see Óolal again?" I asked.

Mack didn't reply immediately, and I felt the air spike with despair. It was really fucking weird.

"I did," he said, sounding solemn. "She must've

heard I was dying and gotten free. The last thing I saw was her beautiful face hovering over mine. I told her I loved her, and then it happened."

"What?"

"It was a whirlwind of screams and fighting and blood and…" He let out a breath. "Her father caught us together and slit her throat two feet from my face, screaming that her disobedience and insults to the gods would bring about suffering for their people."

Oh god. I covered my mouth in horror.

He continued, "I was too weak to do anything but watch the blood pour from her neck. But inside, I wailed in agony. At the same time, Kan screamed violently, cursing me for putting him in the situation to have to kill his own daughter. He said, 'You will forever walk this earth, living my pain.' Of course, all I could hear were Óolal's final words burning deep into my soul. I think that's when I knew that her father's words weren't a threat. They were real. And so were hers."

"What did she say?" I whispered, not aware that I was once again on the edge of my seat.

"She said, 'I will find you. Whatever it takes, my soul will not rest until I find you and set you free.' And then she died." Mack paused for a long moment, perhaps to gather himself before continuing. Meanwhile, I was horrified. "The final irony was that not soon after, more guards from my island—compelled by some mystical homing skills and Mia's orders to keep me safe—showed up looking for me. They'd been but a few weeks behind the Nords the entire time, following our trail. Had they arrived sooner, Óolal would've probably lived. I truly think the gods wanted to punish me."

Chapter Nine

TEDDI

I don't know how long I sat there in silence with Mack, trying to shake off the anguish of the tragedy that had just played out in my mind. It stuck to my skin, permeated my lungs, and rolled around in my stomach with nauseous waves. I literally felt sickened by it.

But why? I'd seen horror movies, read tragic love stories, and I'd played with donor brains in college. I wasn't thin skinned. Okay, yes, I wasn't myself today, all filled up with those annoyingly strange emotions, but this story had somehow worked its way inside me like a rotting splinter, tainting my blood.

"I need to take a breather." I stood and headed for the door, wondering how far I'd get before I vomited. Once outside, I placed my palms against the wall and leaned in. My head was spinning, and my insides twisted with painful cramps.

I suddenly felt someone breathing on the back of

my neck—someone tall from the angle of it. I gasped and turned, finding the entire hallway empty.

"Fuck. What's wrong with me?" I whispered. Suddenly the room began spinning faster and faster, exploding with colors, the walls dripping with blues and reds and…

I can't breathe. I can't breathe. Then the space around me turned dark, and I felt myself falling.

※

Two Days Later.

I dreamed of running down that hill again. Same as the last time. Only, now there were storm clouds above, and the freezing rain pelted my shivering body.

It's not him. It's not him. Dear God, it looks like him, but it's not. All I could think of was getting away, that I'd made some horrible mistake.

I glanced down at my stomach, pressing my hands over a fresh wound, the blood staining the front of my tattered brown dress that looked more like a potato sack. I was going to die, and I knew it. Yet I kept on running. From him. The man with the blue eyes who apparently wasn't who he'd seemed.

I tripped on a rock and flew face-first down the muddy embankment. So much pain. So much pain. I tried to get to my feet but kept slipping.

"You fucking little bitch," said a deep, deep voice from behind me, right before I felt the man grabbing my hair and flipping me over.

"No. Please," I begged for my life.

He stared down at me with disgust and rage, his face covered in blood, those cold blue eyes punching right through my soul.

"You *think* you can take him away from me?" he growled. "You *think* you can rob me of my brother? No one takes what's mine." He raised his other hand and sliced through my neck with a gleaming silver sword.

"Fuck!" I sprang up from my bed, drenched in sweat. *Oh Jesus*. My eyes immediately gravitated toward the night-light in my hallway, visible through the open door. Frantic, I ran my hands over my white pajama shirt, feeling for any wounds.

No, no. I'm safe. I'm home. My plain white dresser and nightstand, the framed picture of my parents hanging over the white armchair in the corner where I read, the sliding door that led out to my redwood balcony overlooking the ocean.

I whooshed out a breath and ran my hands over my face, fully realizing that it had just been a dream. Only this time, everything had been so vivid. Every detail, right down to the texture of the gritty cold mud, the sting of wet wind whipping across my cheeks, the feeling of rot in my stomach.

Fuck, fuck, fuck. I had to get up and try to move around a little. It was now close to midnight, and I'd been in bed for two days, half asleep, half afraid of it. The strange dreams wouldn't stop.

I swung my shaky legs over the edge of the bed and slowly stood, still feeling woozy. I hobbled down the hall, past the bathroom and into the kitchen. I grabbed the glass I kept on the side of the sink and filled it with cold water from the filtered tap.

I chugged and chugged, knowing I'd probably throw it all up like I had everything else the last few days. Much more of this and I'd have to check myself into the hospital for dehydration.

No. You're okay, Teddi. It's just the flu. I'd survive.

I finished my glass and opened the fridge, eyeballing the loaf of bread. *Crap.* I was so hungry, but my stomach wasn't up for entertaining visitors. Luckily, I had reserves, meaning I could never be described as thin because that would require me to care deeply about the opinion of others or my mortality. I never worried about any of that. *Is that all going to change?*

I didn't know, and the only thing that seemed to matter was getting well. I had patients to treat.

You mean Mack.

Okay. I did mean Mack. I'd just run out on him, becoming violently ill after our session. Shannon had driven me home in her car—mine was still at the center.

I stumbled to the bathroom, relieved myself, and then washed my face and brushed my teeth. I always hated feeling filthy, but I felt it even more now. That horrific dream of being covered in blood and dirt had left me wanting a long shower.

If only I could stand up long enough for one.

I got to my bed and slid between the soft sheets,

thankful for the fact that the room had stopped spinning.

"Think you can get away from me that easily, do you?" said a deep voice from the dark corner of the dimly lit room.

"Oh shit!" I jerked upright, and my eyes fixed on the tall figure sitting in the armchair only five feet from the bed. "Who the hell are you?" I instinctively slid the two ends of my collar together, as if closing the front of my PJs could miraculously protect me.

"Don't you recognize me, woman?" He turned on the reading lamp next to the armchair.

Oh shit. Oh shit. Those blue, blue eyes. The same ones from my dreams. But that short black hair and stubble—he was also the man I imagined when Mack described himself in that story. I couldn't sort through this.

"What the hell is going on?" I asked, really talking to myself.

"Allow me to enlighten you, Óolal. My name is King. And like the last five times you've come for my brother, I'm here to stop you. No one takes what's mine."

Óolal?

I blacked out.

Chapter Ten

TEDDI

"Get the hell off her, King!" screamed a woman in the back of my foggy brain.

"You get back in the car. This doesn't concern you, Mia," the man commanded in an authoritative tone that signaled he was used to having his orders followed.

Slap! "Say that one more time, King. I fucking dare you," the woman growled.

"Ow, woman. I swear you test my patience down to the hair on my balls."

"No. You're the one who's testing, because we had a deal. Your evil-cursed-bastard days are over, King. Over. And I didn't go to hell and back to free you just so you could continue tormenting anyone you like. Now step away from that woman or I will get my ass in that car and you won't see me or Archon again."

"You threaten me, wife? I think you forget who I am."

"Forget? How could I forget? Look at you. You're the fucking sexiest man on the planet. I get wet just looking at you."

"Goddammit," the man said, his voice dropping an octave, "I fucking want you. Now." Slurp, slurp, kiss, smack. "Bend the hell over and show me your p—"

I groaned with discomfort. And, okay, disgust. Who the fuck were these people getting ready to get it on with their angry sex in my bedroom? While I was sick as a dog?

"She's awake," the woman whispered. "Put it away."

"No. I'm hard. It must be addressed, Mia. You promised never to leave me wanting."

"Oh, stop it, King. Dammit…look what you made me do."

"Mmmm…Looks good to me."

Smack! "Lactation is not foreplay—you know what? Go. Just go and check on the baby."

"Archon is fine. He's with Arno."

"I don't trust anyone with the last name Spiros," she complained. "Last time I did, I ended up dead. Why did you hire him as your driver again?"

Dead? This had to be a dream.

"Because I am a man," he replied. "One who doesn't ask permission from a woman."

"You went there? Seriously?" She sighed. "Go check on him. Please?" she added sweetly.

"Fine. But this is not over, Mia. And you owe me hot desk sex—"

Desk sex?

"Yes. Fine. It's a deal. Go," said the woman.

"Promise?"

"I'm no welsher—you know that."

"Excellent," he said, his voice filled with lust. "Today is turning out much better than I'd hoped. Except for the part where you didn't allow me to kill my brother's executioner. That part is irritating, and we shall have words tonight." I heard heavy footsteps walking away.

"Honey, can you hear me?" the woman said, a soft hand stroking my cheek.

"Who are you?" I mumbled, trying to get my eyes to focus on the young blonde woman sitting on the edge of my bed. She wore a brown leather jacket and had her hair pulled back, but those were the only real details I could focus on.

"My name is Mia. I'm Mack's sister-in-law."

The Mia from the story? So she was real. Of course, that didn't mean the rest of his story was. "Why are you in my house?"

"We need to find Mack before you do."

Huh? "I don't understand."

"I know you're not feeling well, but we need to know if you've seen him."

"Seen who?" I tried to play stupid.

There was a long pause. "Mack. He's blond, tall, goofy smile, and has those all-American good looks? Lots of tattoos on his arms."

The Mack I knew certainly didn't have a goofy smile. Nevertheless, "Don't know him," I lied. "Why are you in my house?" I repeated.

"Because if we don't find him before you do,

he'll die. For good this time—we know he took off his necklace."

What the ever-fucking-hell did that mean?

"Please, Theodora. Tell me if you've seen him."

I didn't know how to respond and that meant keeping my mouth shut. Perhaps these were the "they" Mack had referred to when he'd said someone was looking for him. In any case, this wasn't making sense. They also didn't seem to know that he was at my facility. So how the hell had they connected the two of us?

"Why do you think I know this man?" I asked. "And why would I want to kill anyone?"

"According to my husband, you've known Mack for over three thousand years. And you always find him. And then you try to kill him. Oh, and you're in love with him, too."

I must be hallucinating again. Or was I?

CHAPTER ELEVEN

TEDDI

The obscenely gorgeous preppy blonde named Mia—possible double for Scarlett Johansson?—heated up some canned chicken soup and made two slices of dry toast, politely commenting on the lack of "anything human to eat in my kitchen," before swearing my illness would pass just as soon as I started accepting the truth.

Truth. Pfft. Clearly, she was on something. And if she wasn't, she needed to be. Something hardcore with an antipsychotic chaser. And if those weren't effective, there was always tequila. For me, of course.

"The same thing happened to me, Theodora. But I promise, it gets better," she'd said.

"What does?" I'd asked.

"Being a Seer. And you have no idea how happy I am to have found you—I think we're the only two left in the world." Then she'd added, "Can't wait to see what gifts you have. Oh—and when you start to see the colors, don't panic. Just let it in." She'd sounded almost giddy about it.

Yes, I'd seen colors on the walls after my session with Mack, like the entire world had been Warholized, but that had been a function of my synapses misfiring due to my nervous system being overloaded.

Seeing no point in arguing with this delusional person, I simply nodded. She then left shortly after, promising to return soon to check on me, also mentioning that I shouldn't be alarmed by her husband, this King man, or the other "large gentleman" who might be standing guard outside my house.

Sure. Nothin' strange or alarming about a man who just threatened to off me (and claimed to have done it multiple times before) standing outside my home, because he thought I was this Óolal person, which, of course, he believed because he was Mack's brother and he and Mack were drinking the same "I'm thousands of years old and from ancient Greece" fruit punch.

Okay. Deep breath.

But as my brain argued and built the case as to why King and Mia were crazy and in need of a jail cell for breaking and entering—him with intent to murder and her with intent to make chicken soup—the other part of my mind kept throwing ugly, vicious curveballs at my poor throbbing skull. Bottom line: Things had been happening to me, and there were no explanations. That dream, for example? King was that man I'd run from. Not *like* him. Not *similar* to him. It *was* him.

What the fuck? I thought, lying there in my bed, staring at the ceiling.

I glanced at the clock on my nightstand. It was just after one in the morning, and I didn't have a car, but I needed to see Mack.

I pulled myself from bed and began digging in my closet. I reached for a long dark sweater, black jeans, and boots. If I really had a guy standing outside my house, my only option was to sneak out the back way. I just hoped no one would be keeping an eye on that part because they assumed I was too sick to go anywhere.

Still feeling queasier than a dog on a boat, I hobbled to the bathroom to pop in my contacts and then grabbed my purse before heading outside through the sliding glass door in the living room. My trembling body creaked its way down the wooden stairs to the beach. *Just breathe, just breathe. You'll be fine.* From there, I'd have to walk about a half mile to the public parking lot and call for a cab.

As I walked along the shore, the night was dark and cold, and the wind felt like icy needles pushing under my skin. I slid my cell from my pocket and called a cab. "Yes, the Carpinteria parking lot."

The woman on the other end probably thought it was a prank because the park was closed after sunset. She asked for my location one more time and helpfully pointed out the time.

"Yes," I said. "I know it's one twenty in the morning. Date gone bad. What can I say?"

The dispatcher immediately changed her snotty tune. I felt bad for appealing to her sense of sisterhood, but desperate times.

While I briefly waited for the cab in the parking lot, I began wishing that the emotional switch inside me hadn't been turned on. I felt afraid and confused and a hundred different things that kept clouding the facts. *How do people live like this?*

The cab pulled up five minutes later, and seven minutes after that, I was at the center, nearly falling to my knees.

If it weren't for my need to conceal my true state from the night watch, I would've given up with the whole standing on my feet thing altogether and crawled my way to Mack. I felt like something was sucking the energy right out of my body.

After dishing a heaping pile of bullshit to the nice security man on duty about a very troubled patient who had me worried, I sauntered down the hall, chin held high, my energy sinking like a brick in a cold river.

When I reached Mack's room, the darkness—for the first time in my life—felt like my sanctuary. Inside that room were answers. Inside that room was Mack, and everything led back to him.

I pushed forward, and my heart sank through the cold floor. The room was empty. *He's gone. He's fucking gone.* I fell to my aching knees, so lost that it hurt more than words could ever express.

They must've found him. They must've taken him away. As I kneeled there, drowning in crippling emotions I wasn't prepared to process, something snapped. My connection to sanity and the world I knew began dissolving.

"I'll fucking kill them," I growled. "I will rip out their goddamned hearts and make them watch."

I mentally stumbled back. None of this was me, yet...it was. The rage, the hate, the power I felt blooming inside with the knowledge that I came equipped to beat down anything or anyone who got in my way.

I rose to my feet, fists clenched, every muscle tensed with raw, potent will. The will to topple, overcome, hit, and kill. *No one will take me down this time. Not fucking King. No one.*

None of this was rational, but it all felt saner than the world I saw in front of me with my own eyes.

I turned and headed to my office, where I grabbed my purse and keys—both had been left there on Monday when I'd fallen ill. I would drive home, park a few blocks away, sneak back inside my house, pack my things, and set out to find Mack.

Wherever he'd gone, I would find him.

How? I just knew I would. Like a magnet pulling itself toward metal. It was just like Mia said. Except for the part about wanting to hurt Mack. To the contrary, I wanted to protect him.

On the way out, I passed by the guard station and informed them that our John Doe had apparently checked himself out. I told them he wasn't a risk to himself so to simply file the paperwork. I didn't want anyone looking for Mack but me.

Five minutes after pulling out of the parking lot, I sat at a lonely red light, thinking about where I'd start my search, when I heard that dark, familiar voice from the backseat of my car. "Head east. I know a place we can go."

"Shit!" I yelped, simultaneously jumping in my seat and swiveling my body to see who the hell was in the back of my car. *Mack?* "*What* are you doing?" I yelled, clutching the fabric of my sweater over my heart. "And how the *fuck* did you get in here?"

He was just sitting there looking completely casual about it—arm resting over the top of the backseat, one leg stretched out. He also wore a leather jacket, and though I couldn't quite make out the style, I imagined he probably looked sexy as hell in it.

"You left your keys on your desk," he said. "I used the remote to unlock the door."

It dawned on me that the question I'd asked was pretty tame compared to all the other monstrosities waiting in line.

"Mack, what the *fuck* is going on?" I barked.

"You mean my brother?"

"Yes! How'd you know?"

"It was only a question of time before he located you—or me—he's very talented at finding things."

What the hell, then? I spat inside my head. "And it didn't cross your mind to warn me? He came to my house to kill me, Mack! Because he said I am going to kill you."

I stared at the large shadow in my backseat, waiting for a reply. It didn't come.

"Well?" I prodded.

"Mia was with him, and I'm sure she made my brother behave. The light is green. Drive east."

"Hell no. Not until you tell me why those crazy assholes broke into my house and said all those things." *And made me soup.*

"It's like you said. They're crazy. And they're looking for me because I took something from them. That's all."

I didn't buy it, but had to ask anyway. "What did you take?"

"The Incan Chalice of Life. I traded it with someone who helped me find you."

Okay. Wasn't expecting that answer.

"May we drive now?" he said.

"Yes. But we're going back to the center." There we could talk under the watchful eye of the security staff.

"You and I both know it won't be safe there. Drive east."

"Why?" I asked.

"Drive east," he insisted.

"Why?" I asked again.

"Because you said you wanted to help me. This is helping me."

I thought it over for a moment. Strangely, that rage-filled voice inside my head from earlier had disappeared. I felt like me again. And good ol' me was saying it wasn't a good idea to just "drive east" with this guy.

"Fine." He reached for the car door and started to exit.

Shit. I couldn't let him go. I couldn't. He was

too…too…well, I wanted to slap myself for saying something so crazy, but he was too important to me. He felt like everything, in fact.

"Okay!" I barked. "I'll drive east."

Mack got back inside and closed the door. "Head for the highway."

I turned toward the steering wheel and started driving east, doing my best to keep my eyes on the road, but taking every chance I had to steal glimpses of the man in my backseat. A proud cheekbone. The full, sensual lips. The strong brow and square stubbled jaw. Each flicker of light from a passing car gave me another peek.

Mack was goddamned beautiful.

Great. Fucking great. He's hot and mysterious. And totally out of his mind.

"Watch out!" Mack barked.

I jerked the car back into my lane and off the shoulder, feeling like a drooling moron.

After a few moments passed, I finally asked, "Any plans to tell me where we're going?"

"Just keep driving." How he'd know that I wasn't the least bit tired or sleepy, I could only guess. But we would drive all night until the sun rose.

Later, I'd look back on the day ahead as the best and the worst day of my life.

Chapter Twelve

MACK

I was torn. Inside and out. Being in the car with Theodora was like being in my own personal hell. How was it possible to want to protect someone and care for them, ache for them and need them, yet feel compelled to harm them *and* want them to kill you, too? *It's downright fucking psychotic. That's what it is.*

Of course, the voice inside my head, screaming to slide my hands around her neck and choke the life from her, wasn't truly mine. It belonged to Óolal's father and his goddamned curse, demanding that I "relive his pain" for eternity. Translated to mean I would feel compelled to kill and then feel guilty as hell about it. The more I cared, the stronger the urge to harm, the bigger the guilt. I supposed that was how he felt about killing Óolal for the good of his people in a quest to not piss off the gods. Idiot. He'd created a monster: Me.

In any case, I wouldn't touch Theodora. I never had, and I never would.

I hoped.

Honestly, we'd never been together for more than a handful of hours at a time. King always got to her somehow. Sometimes before my own heart sensed she was near. Because seeing people for who they once were wasn't a gift I could claim to possess like King. Although I knew that the dead with unfinished business sometimes returned by means of reincarnation or by other unnatural methods, as in my brother's case. In short, he'd been cursed, too, and the moment it was lifted, a cosmic force controlled by the Seers snapped him back to life, righting a wrong that was never meant to be.

As for me, my return was unnatural, as well. A product of multiple forces at work. *But this time, I am going to die, and there will be no return. Theodora will see to it.*

If you don't kill her first.

I quickly barricaded the dark thought behind a wall. A flimsy wall. The clock was ticking.

"Take this off-ramp," I demanded, guiding us to the only place with any hope of preventing King from finding us immediately. His gift of locating people and things was impressive, although what truly made him powerful were the tools in his box. He owned thousands of items—spell books and rare artifacts—that possessed the sort of powers people, especially bad ones, dreamed of possessing. Compelling, untraceable poisons, talismans to drive people mad, gemstones that made one immortal—like the one in the rings King and Mia wore—aphrodisiacs, youth serums—you name it. Add to that, my brother could get inside people's heads and crawl around, well, it made him one scary sonofabitch.

"Are you going to give me a clue where we're going?" Theodora asked.

Still sitting in the backseat, trying to keep my distance and keep my lust at bay—not really working—I replied, "Start looking for a gas station. You're running low."

She was silent on the matter and started searching for a place to pull off the highway. As the sun came up over the horizon directly in front of us, there was a split second where I clearly saw Óolal in the reflection of the rearview mirror. Her long black hair, her wide cheekbones, her full lips. It was only a moment, but it flooded my mind with feelings I'd buried long ago. I closed my eyes, fighting the urge to let them in. I couldn't do this. Not again.

☙❧

TEDDI

When I stopped along the road to get gas and grab a few supplies—water, snacks, and caffeine—I made every attempt to sneak a peek at the man in my backseat, who sadly had his face tilted down and eyes closed.

Seriously? He'd dozed off. I was about to wake him under the guise of needing directions, but really, I just wanted to see his face in broad daylight and gaze into those eyes. What would happen?

Anyway, I stomped down my gnawing curiosity and allowed the man to grab a few minutes of shut-eye, not bothering to wake him until we were back on the highway.

Afterwards, he told me to take a small road north, and we stayed on that for what seemed like forever. Then the green faded. No more trees or grass. Just desert and hills. My best guess was that we were somewhere northeast of Palm Springs and a few hours south of the Mohave Desert.

Mack had me turn down a lonely dirt road that looked like it hadn't been used in years. No fresh tire tracks. No grooves from wear. Just a long flat stretch of golden dirt that disappeared between two hills up ahead.

Just a few meters in, I took my foot off the gas, feeling extremely uneasy. This couldn't be a good idea. Then it hit me again. I felt that door inside my head swing open. Colors began seeping up from the ground. Reds, blacks, and blues swirling together.

Unable to breathe, I stopped the car completely. Then the wave of nausea hit. I put the car into park and bolted out the door, diving to my hands and knees, dry heaving. Nothing came out, but my stomach didn't care.

"Try to relax, Theodora. You're fighting it." I felt a strong, soothing hand on my back.

Mack might as well have been stroking my

breasts or inner thighs or kissing my lips. His touch felt intimate, tender and sensual.

Okay. Feeling better now. In fact, I felt the urge to jump to my feet and kiss him like a long-lost lover I missed with all my heart.

I shook my head from side to side, gathering up my crumbling wits. *Oh look. I'm in the doggy position on the ground with my tongue hanging out. Nice.*

I wiped my mouth with the back of my hand, and Mack gripped my arm to help me to my feet.

This is it, I realized. I was going to turn around and look him straight in the eyes. I already knew how beautiful he was, but the last time we'd locked eyes, it changed me.

His firm grip gently squeezing my upper arm, I slowly turned and gasped. Then my breath stuck in my lungs. *Blue, so blue.* I'd never seen such a stunning set of eyes on a man. And those lips and angular jaw covered in light brown stubble, and the shaggy dirty blond hair falling over his forehead and…

He's so beautiful.

The morning sunlight bathed every masculine feature of his handsome face with soft golden light. I was speechless as he stared down at me.

"What?" he said dryly. "Never seen a three-thousand-year-old man before?" He cracked a sweet smile, and it nearly stopped my heart. Dimples puckered. His eyes lit up. His lips looked like they'd been created for the joy of sex and for laughter and for eating romantic dinners and whispering in my ear while making love and—

Hold the hell on there, Ted. I was not going to sleep with this man. *Yeah, but you want to.* And for someone like me to want someone as badly as I wanted him was complete insanity.

Welp. At least now you can relate to your patients.

I cleared my throat. "I think I'd like to know your beauty regimen," I finally replied to his little wisecrack about his age. Of course, I didn't believe he was that old.

But then, how do I explain all this? I asked myself.

You're a freaking psychologist, Ted. And a woman with a strong brain. That was right. I had to fall back on that. There was a scientific and medical explanation for what was happening here. I was merely getting sucked into these people's occult-like delusions, a victim of my emotions, which were all so new to me.

Still, I couldn't deny the connection I felt with Mack, despite his issues. Luckily, there was no one better equipped on the planet to help this beautiful, crazy man see that he wasn't cursed and he wasn't going to die. And that he, his brother, and that Mia woman were living in some sort of fantasy world. As for the strange coincidence about seeing his brother in a dream, there was a very rational explanation: they'd been watching me. I knew that for a fact. I must've seen this King man somewhere and not realized it.

I almost wanted to slap myself. The colors, the

fainting spells, the emotions I'd been going through were all products of my powerful mind.

Suddenly, I realized Mack was staring down at me, the sunlight reflecting the reddish hues in his blond hair. I found myself loving the way he looked at me, like a cherished object. Then there was the way he looked in general—the way his jeans hugged his strong thighs and the way his plain white tee shirt stretched across his stacked pecs.

"Your green eyes are lovely, Theodora. And the haircut is especially fetching," he said.

Fetching. It was the sort of word nobody used these days, but its charm had my stomach turning into flutters.

I made a little shrug, sweeping my hand over the top of my head, petting my brown bob. "I thought it would make me look more mature."

He huffed out a laugh. "You, of all people, shouldn't worry about that. You're just as old as I am."

Oh, yes. They all think I'm this Óolal woman. I decided now was not the time to start chipping away at his false reality. If I was going to save this man, I'd have to tread carefully and let him see the truth for himself. He was living in a make-believe world.

"I was wondering why my knees always ache when it rains. Must be arthritis." I smiled and followed it with a long breath. "I'm all better now. Should we continue to our destination?"

Mack reached out and stroked my cheek with his rough hands. "I'll drive."

I couldn't move. It felt too good to be touched by him. "O-o-okay."

The slope of his bare arms, with ripped, tattoo-covered biceps, caught the corner of my eye. Mack reminded me of one of those tall, lean, hard Navy SEAL kinds of guys, muscled in all the right places.

"You never told me about those dates and names on your arms," I said.

He dropped his hand and stepped around me, getting into the front seat of my black BMW.

Guess he's not going to answer that.

I watched in awe as he slid the seat all the way back to accommodate his long, muscular legs.

"You getting in, Doctor?" He sat there with a smirk, gripping the steering wheel.

I was staring at him, wasn't I?

"Yep." I nonchalantly made my way around the front of the car, feeling his gaze pinned on me the entire time.

Once inside, he threw it into first and tore down the road.

Chapter Thirteen

TEDDI

"What is this place?" I asked as Mack dug a key from the dirt just beside an old dilapidated cabin out in the middle of nowhere. I couldn't help staring at his large frame as he bent over. Flat stomach—not even a hint of a pooch as he folded himself over; lightly tanned skin—like he'd been somewhere warm and sunny recently; broad shoulders—the kind that told me he wasn't afraid of hard work.

And that ass. Round and hard looking. No man should have such a nice ass. It was unfair to us ladies.

Not wanting him to catch me ogling again, I peeled my eyes away and went back to inspecting the small wooden cabin with the dusty wraparound porch; the entire mess looked like the retired set of an old gunslinger movie. Add to that how this part of the desert wasn't one of those long flat hunks of dirt with cute fork-shaped cactus, but hilly with lots of rocks. Dried-out vegetation and the occasional scraggly tree dotted the hillside, giving the secluded valley the feeling of desolation.

Funny, but I wasn't scared—not even a little—though somewhere in the back of my mind—the one that used to be completely logical but now felt hardwired into my emotions—I realized I was taking a big risk. I should be afraid. I shouldn't have agreed to come to an isolated cabin out in the middle of the desert.

I shouldn't feel what I felt about this man either. But I did.

"Looks like someone detonated an A-bomb here. Everything's dead."

Mack chuckled as he rose to his feet and wiped the dust from his hands on his dark jeans.

"What?" I said.

"We're standing on top of an old Native American burial ground. And they prefer to be called spirits since they're not really dead."

Okay... "Oh. Well, I was referring to the plants. Not the supernatural wildlife—but are you telling me you see ghosts here?"

I hoped he'd say no because I already had my work cut out for me.

He shoved a key into a padlock that was attached to a chain running through a hole in the wood plank door.

"No. I can't see the ghosts. Can you?" He flashed a curious look my way as he fiddled with the rusty lock.

"I don't believe in ghosts."

He turned his head and stared at me for moment

as if I were the crazy one. "You will." He went back to his task and the lock made a pop sound.

Was he trying to frighten me? It wouldn't work.

"How do you know about this place?" I asked.

"I used to be acquaintances with the caretaker in a past life."

I wondered if he meant "past life" figuratively or literally. "So your friend used to take care of an unmarked burial ground. Interesting."

Mack unthreaded the rusted chain through the hole and pushed open the door, giving me a view into the gloomy, dirty interior.

"The dead don't need taking care of," he said. "His job was to keep the living away. But he eventually went insane out here all by himself. Right before he died, he had my brother ward the entire property. It's why you got sick when we stepped onto this land."

I raised a brow. *Ward. Now there's a word you don't hear every day.* It implied that they'd used some sort of voodoo to protect the land.

"I see you don't believe me." He jerked his head, gesturing for me to go inside, which I didn't do. I wasn't afraid, but I also didn't see why we'd want to go in there.

"Why don't you tell me what's inside first?" I folded my arms over my chest, grateful I had on my thick dark sweater. The chill in the morning air was prickly to say the least.

"It's the sort of thing you need to see for yourself." His voice was suddenly tinged with an ominous tone, and I felt the baby fine hairs on my arms and neck stand straight up as the expression on his face shifted into something that was difficult to articulate. It was…like…he wanted to hurt me. Hate. Rage. Whatever. But he looked mean and deadly.

Okay. Now I'm afraid. I realized Mack had my keys and there was nowhere for me to go—nowhere to run, nowhere to hide.

I'm an idiot. If he intended to kill me, which I now had the impression he might, given the strange, deadly vibe oozing from his direction, I deserved to die. Just like those stupid girls who "check out that weird noise" in the attic during a horror movie.

I lifted my chin a bit, faking composure. A victim's fear often fed a killer's ego. "Mack, tell me what you're doing—what's really going on here? Because if you plan to drag me inside to cut my throat, you know I can't go anywhere, so you've won. But I'd at least like an explanation." No. I wasn't giving in. I was buying time to think.

His blue, blue eyes flickered with disdain, and his surreally handsome face was coated in rage. There were no traces of the kind, dimpled man I'd seen only moments earlier.

What the hell happened to him?

"I owe you nothing, Theodora. Now do as I say, and get your ass inside, or I will drag you by the hair."

Oh fuck. I knew in my heart that running wouldn't do any good, but I did it anyway. I turned and sprinted down the road.

Arms pumping, boots slamming into the earth, I

ran as hard as I could, kicking up dirt behind me. I felt a hand grab my sweater and jerk me back. My body slammed onto the ground, knocking the wind from my lungs.

"I fucking told you to get inside, woman," Mack growled as I tried to breathe but couldn't. With little effort, he plucked me from the dirt and threw me over his shoulder.

My lungs kicked back in, and I screamed, "Don't do this, Mack! I can help you. You don't want to do this!"

Marching with determination, me bouncing painfully on his shoulder, he said, "Shut the hell up. You have no clue what I want to do."

I clawed and kicked, but he was too burly, and I was no match. "Mack, please! I'm begging you to let me—"

We crossed the threshold into the cabin, and that was when I became pretty darn certain that I was the one who'd gone mad.

Chapter Fourteen

TEDDI

"What the…?" I whispered.

Mack threw me down onto a soft leather couch beside an unlit fireplace, and then gripped the sides of his head, snarling and groaning with his eyes closed as if in pain. Then suddenly his face relaxed and his head snapped in my direction. "You cannot run from me like that, Theodora. Do you understand me? Do you!" he yelled.

Nodding absentmindedly, I was totally speechless. The inside of the cabin wasn't dark and dusty, and the walls weren't rotting wooden planks. The inside was rustic, yes, but it had clean white plaster walls and a cozy living room with a bearskin rug, fireplace, and knotted pine coffee table. In the other corner was a round table with a gas lamp in the middle and a hutch filled with canned food, stemware, and plates. There was even a little kitchen area with a propane hotplate and a granite counter.

My mouth half flapping, I stuttered out, "I—I—dun-dun-don't understand." And then I looked up at Mack. "Holyfuckingshit!" I was no longer looking at him, but...but... "Your hair. Your face." His hair was dark, his stubble was jet black, his skin was a deep olive. But those eyes—those blue, blue eyes. He looked like that man King. Exactly like him.

Mack stood there, arms crossed, staring.

"Mack? Please help me understand what's happening here."

"You are a Seer, Theodora. And these grounds—think of it as a place where the energy you draw your gifts from is concentrated."

He meant to say it was turbocharging me or something. The crazy thing was, I could feel it. I could feel this strange pulse beating through my veins and throbbing against the inside of my skin.

He continued, "It's why the tribe who once lived here considered it sacred."

"But you don't look like you, and this place is not what I saw when you opened the door."

"A spell to trick the eye and keep people from coming inside just in case they make it past the wards around the edge of the property," he added.

"So...you..." I blew out a breath. Mack looked so...so...fucking goddamned beautiful. I had to look away and try to process.

"You're seeing me as I once was when we first met," he explained. "Don't you remember me?"

I shook my head no.

He reached over onto the hutch and grabbed a small silver ashtray. "I don't have a mirror, but this will do. Look at yourself."

I took it from him and glanced at the shiny surface. The blurry reflection staring back wasn't the face I knew in the mirror.

"Shit!" I dropped the thing on the floor. The eyes had been brown and almond shaped with thick black lashes.

My mind fought against it all because it wasn't possible. Not one single bit of it. Yet, there it was. Proof. Standing right in front of me. Still, I couldn't quite swallow such a big ugly pill. Because if all this wasn't a fantasy, then that meant all of the stuff Mack and his brother had told me might be real, too.

"I, uhhh…" I stood from the couch. "I need a moment. Outside. Alone," I added.

Mack gave me a look, and once again I had to avert my eyes. Seeing a face different from the one I knew made my insides churn like miserable mules tethered to an old flour mill.

"I won't run," I told him. "Besides, where would I go?"

"Make it quick. We don't have much time before they find us."

"Your brother, you mean," I said.

"He's not the only one looking for me."

"Oh goodie." I turned for the doorway and pulled the handle. "I'll be right outside. Please ignore the screaming."

I stepped onto the dusty old porch that creaked under my weight and then flashed a glance over my shoulder. Once again, I saw nothing inside except for cobwebs, dirt, and rotting wood plank walls.

I shut the door. Walked a few yards away and screamed at the top of my lungs.

※

After my initial shock subsided, Mack and I settled in with our meager supplies, and he built a small fire in the fireplace to take the chill from the air. As for me, I had so many questions leapfrogging inside my head that I really didn't know where to start. There was the part about my being a Seer. Was my mother one, too? Or anyone else in my family? Then there was Mack. He really was three thousand years old.

Crazy.

And people really were looking for him. And I really had been murdered by that King guy, reborn over and over again.

Crazier.

Overnight I'd gone from being a person who lived in a world defined by logic, to a person living in a world where logic was completely useless. The old Teddi—focused and analytical, who was probably smarter than the average bear because her world had once been free of emotional distractions—she was dead. Or more accurately stated, she was buried deep underneath layers and layers of the real me.

But who was I?

Unfortunately, that question would have to wait. Because Mack still believed he had to die, and I wanted him to live. Of that, there was no question.

After snacking on some jerky and chugging a big bottle of water, I settled down on the couch, and Mack took the old-fashioned-looking leather armchair in front of the fire. I couldn't stop staring at him. That jet black hair falling over his ears, the black eyebrows and whiskers on his sculpted jaw. It was strange how different he looked, less all-American-hotty-slash-special-forces poster boy and more like a man whose beauty was truly from another time. Exotic, I guess I'd call him.

"You'll have to stop staring," he said, gazing into the fire. "It's making me feel self-conscious." He cracked a sweet little smile, and it was just as infectious as the smile I'd seen earlier.

"I can't help it. It's just that…you're so…" I wanted to say fucking hot, but instead said, "different."

"It's an illusion. A reflection from your memories."

"So I'm really this Óolal person," I said.

"You still don't remember?"

I shook my head, and he made a little *hmph!* sound.

"Did you expect me to?" I asked.

"You usually remember something—sometimes all at once, sometimes in bits and pieces, but you remember eventually."

"And have you always introduced yourself in such a mysterious manner?" I asked, referring to the dark room at the clinic.

"No. Looking at you is…I was trying to

avoid…never mind. It doesn't matter."

His response only piqued my curiosity. I had assumed that the dark room was because he didn't want me to see him, but perhaps it had been the other way around. "Is it because you and I were once…" I swallowed the words I'd meant to say.

"I loved you," he said.

"And now?"

"It's complicated," he replied.

"No kidding." I held my hands out toward the fire to soak in a little more heat. It was the middle of the day, but it was also still February.

He glanced at me, frowning. "These days, love is something people see in movies or on television, a fantasy concocted by the media they try to mimic. Their version is fleeting and cheap."

"Not true. My parents love each other. They've been together for forty years."

"Because they likely have a unique connection—a rarity that goes beyond today's definition of love."

"What about you and me?" Obviously I didn't love him. I barely knew the guy. Or…I did and—never mind. I had no fucking clue what was going on.

"You and I have a connection, too. Only ours was forged in a moment of torment and pain."

"Care to elaborate?" I said.

"It's simple. Your father was a powerful man, and he cursed me to roam the earth, living his pain of having to kill you. You are also very powerful and didn't want that, so your soul won't rest until you've released me from your father's curse. Which is why you must kill me—you're the only one who can free my soul."

I cringed.

"Don't look so shocked," he said.

"I think you're misinterpreting my lack of enthusiasm. And you're mistaken if you think I'm going to kill you."

"You have no choice, Theodora. It's your fate. And you want to be free of your vow just as much as you want to free me."

"Fuck you. I won't kill you."

"Sooner or later, I will not be able to hold back. That rage you saw out there—that violent man—he's inside me. And looking at you only aggravates him. Eventually, he'll break free again, and when he does, he'll try to kill you. You will have no choice but to defend yourself and end me."

I understood now what he was saying, nevertheless… "There has to be another way."

He gave me a look that made me want to crawl inside a hole and die. "What?" I snapped back.

"You think I haven't tried?"

"How the hell should I know? Not like I've had time to think through every piece of this."

"My brother and I have attempted to break the curse many times—nothing works. Not even dying. And, by the way, the part where I'm dead, disembodied, no way to feel anything other than suffering and pain, that's no picnic. You have to do this for me, Theodora. You are just as powerful as your father was, which means you are capable of ending this pain. And you must do it now. Before I lose control and try to hurt you."

I understood what he was saying. I truly did. Seize the moment. But I could not do what he asked. I wasn't capable of murdering someone. I just wasn't.

"I'm sorry, but we're just going to have to wait until you 'lose control,' because I'm not about to take a knife and slit your throat or run you over with my car or whatever the hell you imagined I'd be doing to you."

Mack shook his head at the floor. "If I get to you first, then all this starts over again. You'll be reborn, and I will have to sate my urges."

I stared at him, trying to grasp what he was saying. He didn't mean that…that… "You go around killing people?"

"I'm very good at it."

I wanted to vomit. I didn't remember my father, this Kan man, but what a jackass. What was he thinking when he'd cursed Mack?

"Great. You're a serial killer."

"No. Never that. But there is always killing to be done in this world, Theodora. For my brother, for powerful people, for pride and country."

I just…I just… "This is too much." I stared at him in complete wonder. And awe. And then the lust kicked in.

One corner of his mouth curled into a wide smile.

"What?" I asked.

"Nothing. You gave me that same look the second time we met."

"I wish I could remember," I said.

"Perhaps you simply don't wish to. Not a surprise, frankly."

I was in no position to speculate. "Tell me what you remember. I want to know everything." What I really wanted to know was how to save him. And the devil was always in the details.

"If I tell you, will you do what I've asked?" he said.

I couldn't lie, so I danced around the question. "It might increase your odds of persuading me."

He shook his head. "Stubborn. You are always so stubborn."

☙❧

MACK

It was the least I could do for Theodora, I supposed. By my estimations we still had a few hours left until King used his gifts to find us and until the deed needed to be done. And I had to admit, spending time with her, staring into her large green eyes (I wasn't a Seer, so I saw the real her), watching the way she looked at me, it all started bringing back those memories from when she was Óolal and I was simply a stranded stranger in her village.

So yes, even against my better judgment and knowing how much more difficult it would make Theodora's task of ending me, I found myself unable to resist having these final moments together. There was nothing sweeter, nothing more right in this world than spending time with her. When I wasn't busy pushing back my urge to kill her, that was.

I cleared my throat, determined to project nothing but confidence. There could be no doubt in her mind regarding how this day would end.

"The second time we met," I said, "was about five hundred years ago. I had been recently raised from the dead by my brother after his many failed attempts. Not a happy period of my life—King was as tormented, bloodthirsty, and just as violent as I was. And he was strong—something he liked to remind me of."

I watched Theodora's expression sour. "He hit you?"

"No. He *beat* me. Severely. But he beat anyone who displeased him. He killed anyone who disobeyed him."

"Jesus. No wonder you don't want to see the guy."

"I admit that I dreamed of killing my brother and taking revenge, but then I learned the truth about him and what he'd given up to bring me back from the dead."

"Don't hold me in suspense," she said with a certain grim fascination.

"He was cursed like I was, but he was a ghost, his soul in constant pain."

Theodora's mouth sort of hung open, revealing a bit of that soft pink tongue. I wanted to stroke it with mine along with a few of her other body parts.

I shifted in my chair so she wouldn't notice my

arousal. "I had to hand it to my brother; his sheer will to get back to Mia was a force unlike any other. Though it took him a few centuries, he learned how to materialize for short instances. From there, he began tracking down people—shamans, witches, Seers, anyone with gifts who could help him extend, control and manipulate the curtain that separated him from the world of the living. He got so good at it that no one knew he was dead. He amassed a huge fortune and built a powerful network of very dangerous allies; he could go anywhere he wanted with the blink of an eye. But when he finally found a way to bring me back into this world, he gave up the opportunity for himself."

"So he could've brought himself back to life but didn't."

"Yes. He chose me over his own needs. He said that without me by his side, he would never be able to set his life right again."

"I'm still unclear about how one comes back from the dead and gets a new body."

I shrugged. "It took him a few thousand years to do it—he found a man who knew how to use a particular necklace he obtained many, many years prior from Cleopatra."

"How'd he get a necklace from her?"

"He fucked her, gained her trust, and once he got his hands on it, he killed her."

Theodora's face twisted with disgust. "Remind me to stay far the hell away from your brother."

"Don't feel bad for her. Cleopatra was ruthless and powerful. She had plenty of blood on her own hands."

"I always thought she died from a snake bite."

"A myth. She died from having her body drained of blood—something that my brother also wanted since it fetched a high price on the black market."

Theodora frowned.

"Cleopatra was no ordinary woman," I explained. "She was so powerful that ingesting just a few drops of blood could make a person look ten years younger."

"How do you know all this?"

"I have helped my brother run his business, on and off, for centuries." Ironic, I know. I had been dead set against ever working with him, but some things were simply meant to be.

"What does he do?" she asked.

"He's a power broker of sorts, but the occult version."

"I'm definitely staying away from him."

A wise choice. "Well, the issue is that he and I are linked. Our souls connected as twin brothers."

I could see the dots connecting inside Theodora's mind.

"That's why he refuses to let you die," she whispered, clearly thinking aloud.

"Like I said, your modern definition of love pales in comparison to mine. Love, real love, when you cherish the soul of another above your own, whether it's family, friend, or lover, that bond is difficult to sever. It's why my brother never gave up trying to bring me back. When he failed after hundreds of attempts, he finally understood that my body was the key. Cleopatra's ankh necklace couldn't produce a new one, so he had to find a body for me."

"I really don't want to know how he did that because I'm guessing I wouldn't like that story. But, he did choose nicely." She supplied a weak smile.

I understood that Theodora was trying to make light, but the displaced soul, the young man who used to own this shell, had his life torn away. It was one more pebble on the heaping pile of guilt that comprised my existence.

"The necklace stopped me from aging past a certain point and kept me from dying from that day forward," I added.

"Wow. That's a very impressive necklace. Are you wearing it now?"

"No. King made sure it wasn't easy to remove; I had to pay a very high price to have it taken off." The Incan chalice I stole from my brother was intended to bring back Mia's dead brother. Unfortunately, I needed something to barter with so I could get help finding Theodora. I also needed help removing that necklace—otherwise, my body would just keep coming back.

"So you said that you and I met a second time. Where? When?" she asked.

I could tell from the twinkle in her eyes she was expecting a romantic story of two lost souls searching for one another. But nothing could be further from the truth.

CHAPTER FIFTEEN

MACK

1512

We were savages. No question about it. My brother, King, was building his empire of power and honing his abilities to walk among the living while he searched for the Artifact—the stone he needed to break his own curse and get his life back. As for myself, I had been resurrected but was going out of my mind after wandering the earth as a tormented soul for more than two thousand years.

Nothing made sense to me except pain and killing. It was why, after I slaughtered his entire household of servants—thirty-three maids of all ages, the youngest sixteen, along with forty-nine guards—my brother had to do something. Not that he cared about my killing his staff. He was more concerned about my drawing the wrong type of attention.

"You need time to get this out of your system,

Callias," King said, pacing the length of his lavish study at his French villa in Marseille that overlooked the ocean. "Meanwhile, I will deal with the cleanup and take care of the local authorities."

I sat on the cream-colored silk couch next to the fire, dripping with blood. Hell no. I didn't care about the couch. All I could hear were the screams of my victims and the voice in my head telling me to do it again.

"What have you done to me, Draco?" I growled in agony.

"Shut your mouth, brother. Let me think."

I stood up, ready to make him my next victim. "Why did you bring me back?" I couldn't believe what I'd done. The absolute horror of it all. Nevertheless, those brief moments of peace I'd experienced after taking each life had felt like a small piece of sanity. Heaven. Calm. Bliss.

"Must you ask?" He casually tugged on the sleeve of his white blousy shirt. The people of these times dressed so oddly, the men in velvety tunics gathered at the waist and the women in their giant skirts. These were not the free-flowing gowns of my time.

"It was wrong, Draco. Wrong when I took your head. Wrong when I died. Wrong when you brought me back to life." Though I knew he'd resurrected me for purely selfish reasons, so no, I didn't have to ask why he'd done it. Nevertheless, "Nothing good will ever come of you or me."

"I said be quiet," he barked.

"Or what? You'll slay me?"

He shook his head and began mumbling. "Never. We are twins, one soul divided into two bodies."

It was what he believed at the time. Later, we'd evolve. Though we were connected, we were two different souls, two different bodies, one original set of DNA. But science was just as much a mystery to us back then as it was to anyone.

"I'm sending you to find the Artifact," he said. "You'll pick up the trail where you last saw it and see where it leads you."

For all I knew, the Artifact was back in Greece. My guards had shown up right before I'd died, and I'd asked them to take it to Mia.

"How do you propose I get back to…to…the place I died?" Memories of Óolal flashed through my mind. I couldn't quite make sense of them.

"I have given money to a Diego Velázquez de Cuéllar, a Spaniard who has been charged with establishing a settlement on an island called Caobana, not too far from where you perished. You will sail with him."

"He works for you?" I asked.

My brother smiled. "They work for gold, which I have plenty of. Therefore, everyone works for me. You will tell him you are there to oversee my investment and help locate objects for my collection."

And so the next day, I set out on horseback to Spain to deliver the letter and travel on this ship to the New World. Four and a half months later, I had arrived to the place once occupied by Óolal's people, only to find a jungle abandoned long ago.

Any traces had been consumed by vegetation. But I didn't give a shit. Those few months, traveling in this world that was so changed yet so similar to the one I'd left behind, made me feel like a kid in a candy store. Killing was my candy, and there were plenty of people deserving of it. I killed thieves on the road to Spain who'd tried to take my horse. I killed a drunk group of men who were beating a woman outside of a brothel near the port. I killed several men who'd tried to overthrow the ship. It was when I learned how my darkness and willingness to kill could serve another purpose. I was a man who couldn't die. I didn't know fear. I was consumed with a need to shed blood. Every time I obeyed that need, it felt like a drug. Then guilt would kick in, and then I'd kill again for relief. Nevertheless, I believed I'd found my calling.

When we reached Caobana, now known as Cuba, it felt like my own personal heaven. The indigenous population was in need of some taming, and I was in need of some killing.

We hadn't been there more than five days when Diego started gathering men to fight an uprising.

Of course, he asked me to lead. "You're an animal, Callias. And a fine warrior. You will clear the way for our settlement. Show these heathens no mercy."

The next morning, armed with swords, myself and a group of men invaded a small village about one mile south of the port. I remember bursting into the first hut, the blood pumping through my veins, calling for my sweet, sweet drug. But when my eyes met those of the young woman kneeling in the corner, wearing only the traditional loincloth, shielding two small children, I froze. My eyes saw Óolal. It was only for a moment, but it was real. And if I'd had any doubts, they were dispelled by the sweet smell of her permeating the small dwelling.

"It can't be," I said.

She looked at me, her eyes filled with shock. I didn't speak her language, but when that familiar voice filled the air, I fell to my knees, my sword dropping with me. Her presence was ten times more potent than any kill I'd ever made.

I don't know how long we stayed there staring at each other—confused, elated, horrified, and happy—but the screams outside woke me.

"I have to get you out of here." I held out my hand, and she took it, urging the two children to follow.

I looked outside to scout for the rest of the men, who were off inside the other dwellings, killing.

"Come. Hurry!" I said.

They followed me along the outer perimeter of the hut and into the jungle. Meanwhile my head pounded and spun. Could this really be her?

If not for the noise in my head, I probably would've heard the footsteps coming up behind us. When I turned to see why Óolal and the children had stopped following, it was too late.

That day would forever be known as the massacre near Camagüey. But what the history books do not tell is that I was the one doing the massacring. Spaniards, indigenous people, anyone who crossed my path. I was blinded with rage.

When the Spaniards finally caught up with me, I let them kill me. I wanted my pain to end.

But it wouldn't.

Cleopatra's ankh brought me back a few days later, and I clawed my way out of a mass grave, stole a boat, and headed north. I was beyond psychotic—something that wouldn't change for the next several hundred years.

CHAPTER SIXTEEN

TEDDI

I wanted to judge Mack for the crimes he'd committed. I wanted to wish him to hell and make sure he stayed there. But the fact that he truly hadn't been in control steered my heart in another direction: pity.

To be frank, I wasn't a religious person. Not because I didn't want to be, but because my analytical mind had never been able to subscribe to anything without proof. But if there was a god, she had abandoned this poor man long ago and left him to rot. It wasn't fair. I could see the torment in his eyes, hear the guilt in every syllable spoken from his mouth, feel the despair leeching into the air around him. If there was a god, why punish him like this? Because he'd killed his brother? Mack had done it, thinking he might save their people. For screwing me without my father's permission? Mack said he'd loved me. For becoming cursed with my father's pain or being resurrected by his brother? Or because he wasn't strong enough to resist their will?

This man didn't choose. He was forced into every action. Yet he took the blame for all of it.

"Your guilt, Mack, is a sign that you are *not* evil," I said.

As he stared at the crackling fire, I could tell his mind was off in some other world, reliving his sins.

"Mack," I snapped, bringing him back, "you need to listen to me. You are not responsible for whatever you've done."

He speared me with his gaze. "You don't get it, do you? That doesn't matter. Because at the end of the day, I am the one who has to live with the memories. I see their faces. I hear their cries. I relive their pain. What the fuck does guilt have to do with any of it? I just want it to stop."

"If I'm this person you say I am, then we can figure out a way to end the curse. And I can help you with the memories, too, Mack. I can work with you like I do all my patients."

"You still don't remember me, do you?" he snapped.

"Don't change the subject—"

"Answer me," he demanded.

I didn't see where he was going with this, but fine. "No. I don't remember. But what does that matter?"

"It matters because you always remembered. Sometimes it took a while, but you did. And this time, I passed you on the street. We were two feet apart and you didn't even look in my direction."

"You mean before you checked into the center?"

"That was when I knew; even you had recognized that it was time to give up. On me. On us. It is time to move on. And that is why I approached you the way I did, without trying to reignite what we had or felt, Theodora. I just needed your instincts, your curse to kick in so you'd kill me. But this—us." He toggled his finger between us. "This needs to end."

"Well, I'm sorry, but you're wrong. Dead wrong. I'm not *even* close to giving up, Mack. Not even a little."

Slowly, the human warmth in his eyes faded. He bolted from the armchair and threw me down onto the floor.

"Don't fucking argue with me, you bitch," he growled, pinning me by the neck. "You did this to me. You fucking had to offer yourself, didn't you, Óolal? And you knew all along what would happen."

Clawing at his hands, I choked out the only words I thought would reach him. "Okay. You win," I croaked. "I'll kill you."

Slowly, he released his grip around my neck, and the expression on his face turned to shock. "Fuck." He scooped me up and pulled me into his broad chest. "Fuck, fuck, fuck. Are you all right?"

Panting and grateful for the ability to do so, I nodded frantically, my face pressed against his heaving chest. "I'm okay." But now, more than ever, I was determined to save him. I didn't want him to die. He deserved to find peace and live the life I'd robbed him of.

Slowly, Mack pulled back and stared into my eyes, the firelight dancing in his pupils. "Did you mean what you just said? You'll do it?"

Oh God. I didn't want to lie to the man, but I had to. He had to see I was on his side. All I needed was to understand how to undo this horrible curse, and perhaps a part of me already knew. I just had to bring it to the surface.

More time. I need more time.

"I meant it," I lied. "But I want something for it."

Cradling me in his arms, Mack's troubled gaze drifted to my lips, and though that wasn't even close to what I'd planned to propose, I found myself sitting there thinking, *Yeah, that'll work, too.* Heck, more time was more time, right?

He smiled in a consoling kind of way, the dark hair falling into his vivid blue eyes. "The first time I saw that same look in your eyes, you got me into a hell of a lot of trouble, woman."

I couldn't help it. I just couldn't; my heart was racing all over the place and swooning like crazy. Yes, for a man who'd tried to strangle me only moments earlier. But now…God, that look on his face, so hypnotically seductive, so mind-numbingly raw and sweet and so…

Goddamn mine. I slid one hand behind his neck and pulled his mouth to mine. Our lips collided with what felt like an electric spark that rippled through the air. Was this what people meant when they talked about love sometimes feeling like being hit by a bolt of lightning? Whatever the case, I couldn't deny what I felt inside my soul, a need so deep I never wanted to let him go.

I poured myself into the kiss and savored the roughness of the masculine stubble surrounding two satiny lips.

Of course, kissing this man would feel like that: a sinful contrast. Rough and soft.

He languidly slid his lips over mine, as if also enjoying the texture, and then placed a gentle kiss on the corner of my mouth.

Ohmygod. The sinful sweetness of that did me in. I'd been kissed before, but there'd never been any emotion in it for me. But the two of us, just breathing each other in, pressing our mouths softly together, spoke directly to my heart. The way he carefully kneaded his lips against mine and held me to him, as gentle as ever…So irresistible.

Perhaps he didn't want to frighten me. Perhaps he was merely testing the waters, making sure that switch inside him wouldn't flip. I didn't know, but there was no way a man who took so much care to kiss me like this was evil. Wickedly seductive, yes. But not evil.

With my hand still threaded into the silky hair at the back of his neck, I pushed my mouth firmly to his and ran my tongue over his plump bottom lip, urging him to give me more.

And he did.

His gentleness subsided, and his eagerness exploded. His tongue slid between my lips and stroked and pushed and lapped against my mouth, as if desperate to get inside me.

Ohgod. His smell and taste were so delicious.

The feel of him, the heat of him, the shape of his powerful arms holding me to him. I could see why I wasn't able to resist this man three thousand years ago. Everything about him was pure seduction.

The two of us kissing like wild hormone-riddled teenagers, he lowered me to the floor and stretched his long, hard body against the length of mine. The bearskin rug beneath us was warm and soft, just perfect for ripping off our clothes and going at it, but I could tell immediately that wasn't Mack's plan. He was trying to stay in control. I could also tell he was gifted in the lovemaking department, which was why a big part of me wanted him to let go. I'd waited my entire life to feel something like this and to feel it with Mack...there was nothing my body wanted more.

His warm hand slid underneath my shirt, and his fingertips teasingly stroked the soft skin just beneath my breasts, but he didn't move to touch them.

This is torture. Delicious torture. The way he pressed his body against mine, but wouldn't allow me to feel his arousal. The way his mouth moved with mine in teasing, rough kisses. He was in control right now, control over me, and he liked it that way.

But I wanted more. I needed more.

I shifted my body at an angle and wrapped my leg around his hip, pulling him closer, inviting him to slide between my legs. I wanted to feel that hard cock locked away inside his jeans.

He denied my request by unwrapping my leg and

then grabbing my wrists, pushing them into the rug, holding me in place. I responded by pushing my breasts into his chest and kissing him harder. He replied by sliding his mouth down my neck and sucking and licking the sensitive skin just above my collarbone.

Oh, God. He's trying to drive me mad. His short whiskers tickled deliciously while his mouth massaged and kneaded, helping me imagine what that tongue of his might be capable of if working on my hard nipples or throbbing c-spot.

A soft moan escaped my mouth. "What are you doing?" I whispered toward the ceiling, panting.

"Mmmm…" He slid his hand underneath my shirt again, and his nimble fingers worked down my bra just enough to make my breasts spill out over the top.

I gasped when his hand cupped the soft flesh. Every little thing he did felt amplified and exaggeratedly sensual. Was it because I'd never had real emotions before while being intimate? No, it was definitely this man.

"Was it like this our first time?" I whispered as he bathed my neck and the corners of my mouth in a flurry of kisses.

Suddenly, he stopped.

"What's wrong?" I looked up at those stunning blue eyes peering at me from behind a curtain of shaggy black hair.

"You really want to know?" he said.

I nodded. "Yeah, I do."

"Being with you ruined me for all other women.

And it was the happiest moment of my life."

I swallowed hard and tried to stop my eyes from tearing up, but it was useless.

"Why does that make you sad?" he asked, his voice low and deep.

"Because I can't remember it."

He smiled at me, brimming with cockiness. "Perhaps you need your memory jarred."

Suddenly, all these feelings welled up deep inside my chest. If I had to take a stab at identifying what it was, I'd have to say love.

Yes, I loved him. Overwhelmingly, desperately, and deeply.

I just didn't know what to do with that. I had no experience whatsoever with needing someone and wanting them as much as this.

Crap. I can't do this. I was in way over my head here.

Panic set in. I slid his hand off my chest and slowly sat up.

"I don't blame you," he said, misreading my actions. "I wouldn't want to risk it with a madman either."

I glanced down at him. He had his head propped up with one arm and was lying on his side. He looked so relaxed. So ruggedly sexy with his long, hard, lean frame stretched across the rug.

"It's not that." I wanted him more than I'd ever wanted anything.

"I hope you're not going to leave me hanging."

I got up and sat back on the sofa, leaning forward with my face in my hands. I didn't want to tell him what was going through my head even though I doubted it would shock him. "I think we should just—"

"Now I insist you tell me." I could hear the irritation in his voice. "Or is it that you're too good to share your thoughts with someone you see as damaged. I'm still your patient in the back of your mind."

"What? No," I snapped, dropping my hands. "I mean, yes, I want to help you. But I don't think I'm too good." If anything, I felt the opposite. If I wasn't able to cope with my feelings at this juncture, I certainly wasn't going to fare any better if we were intimate. And now that I'd thought about it, I was probably incapable of pleasing him anyway. To me, sex had been little more than a physical activity I performed with my boyfriend because it was required to keep him happy. Of course, it hadn't. He'd ended up fucking my best friend to supplement his needs.

"Then?" Mack asked.

I blew out a breath. "It's not easy to explain."

"You seem to have a gift for working through difficult conversations. I suggest you rely on that fancy PhD of yours."

"I, uhhh…Well, before I met you, I had a condition."

He sat up and twisted his body to face me, placing his back against the armchair. "Go on."

"I wasn't able to really feel anything. Not like I do now."

He folded thick arms across his broad chest. "Feel how?"

I shrugged. "Emotions. I didn't have any. It was like that part of me was broken. I mean, I understood when situations were good or bad, and I knew the appropriate reaction—to smile because someone did something nice for me, to laugh when someone told a joke, to stay serious when someone said something sad, but I never really felt anything. I was just…numb." I looked over at Mack, and he had the most peculiar expression on his face, like he was trying to figure something out.

"And now?" he asked.

"The moment our eyes met, that door was kicked wide open. You fixed me."

He pursed his lips and scratched his rough chin, producing a bristly sound I found oddly sensual.

"I don't know. Maybe…" his voice trailed off, and he shook his head. "I really don't have a fucking clue."

"When you met me any of those other times, was I like that?"

"No. You were normal. I mean to say—you-normal, not normal-normal. You are, after all, extraordinarily unique and beautiful regardless of the body you inhabit. You're also a Seer," he added.

His comment made my toes tingle. I'd never felt adored before now. "Well, I really don't feel like anything other than ill equipped to handle this entire situation."

"Trust me, you are powerful. And you're equipped to handle anything. Even me." He flashed the sweetest smile I could ever hope to see on a man—wicked or not.

As I basked in the glow of that, the wheels started turning. Mia had said something about my having undiscovered gifts. The only thing I'd ever seen was that I had a very strong knack for diagnosing illnesses, not just in the psychology field either. I remember when I was five, my grandfather kept complaining of being tired. I told him his heart wasn't giving him enough blood. I don't know why I'd said that, other than it had somehow seemed obvious to me. My poor grandfather had a heart attack three days later. Luckily he survived and lived another ten years.

Mack went on, "Seers are connected to that part of world that cannot be seen with the naked eye—the energy all around us, the light that makes up the soul, etcetera. You can draw from it and use it in ways that defy the laws of nature in *this* world. It's not unheard of for a Seer to time travel."

"Damn. I feel cheated. The only thing I've gotten out of this is having dreams about your brother hunting me down like an animal. At least, I think it's him."

Mack groaned. "Fucking King. If only you knew how many times we went at it because of you."

"Really?" I don't know why it surprised me, but it did.

"Really. Somehow, he'd sense when you were back and getting near to finding me. And then he'd hunt you down and kill you."

"But why did he think I would come after you

like that? I mean, look at me now."

"He never said. Perhaps he feared I would beg you and you would be guilted into releasing me—like now."

I did feel an unstoppable need to save him, but I had zero desire to kill him. *I think they're operating under a huge misconception.* If anything, earlier back at the hospital, I'd wanted to kill anyone and everyone but Mack. I felt protective of him.

He continued, "I always knew King did it out of his own distorted sense of love for me, and, of course, I felt as guilty as hell that he'd given up his chance to truly live again for me. But there were quite a few centuries where I stayed as far away as I could from him."

"Where did you go?"

"Anywhere that I thought my skills might be useful. I fought in almost every war you could imagine—the Civil War, both World Wars, Korea—I followed the blood. I flew planes and helicopters, manned gunning stations, served in the infantry, drove tanks—I've done it all."

It was an oddly patriotic way to make lemonade out of his situation.

"It wasn't until the Gulf War that I finally gave it up," he said.

"Why?"

"I was in charge of torturing prisoners. Three hundred and sixty-eight people experienced my handiwork. One day, I was overseeing the interrogation of a woman not much older than you are now. I remember thinking to myself that I knew she was hiding something. I could see it in her eyes. The two men in my command weren't making any headway, so I took over. And there was a moment when she screamed that I woke up and realized where I was and what I was doing. Almost like I'd been in a daze for centuries. I was so sick, so disgusted with myself that I walked out and never looked back.

"Afterwards, I was lost for a few years. I don't remember much other than I traded my freedom to a woman who had a very special gift and could make me forget in exchange for…my services."

"By services, I'm guessing you mean sexual favors." I saw no need to beat around the icky bush on that one.

"More than that. She kept me tied up in her basement. King finally found me and bartered for my freedom, but I was gone. Mentally gone. It took him another few years to bring me back. But he never gave up."

"He really loves you." I suddenly found myself conflicted about this King man. As for the rest of Mack's story, it would take a lifetime—perhaps more—to truly digest what it meant to fight and kill like he had. It was just too damned…complicated.

"My brother does love me," Mack said. "Which was why I did everything I could to help get his life back. Now, he's alive, free of his curse, has Mia by his side, and a baby son."

There. That was it! The key to getting Mack to hope again. A little light had flickered in his eyes just then as he'd told me about his brother's new life. He felt good about it. Perhaps it was something he even wanted for himself.

"If your brother was cursed and not such a nice person, I can imagine he has difficulties letting go of the past."

Mack shook his head. "Everyone always thinks I'm the nice brother, the good one. But compared to me, King is a goddamned saint. I've killed thousands of people, Theodora."

I looked down at my hands, letting that sink in. "Most of them were in wars."

"Does it matter?"

"Yes. Because if you think you're a monster for killing men during war, then logic would say that every person who has ever killed for their country is also unworthy of living. I'm sure that's not how you feel."

"I killed because it made me feel good. Not because I gave a shit about politics or felt a patriotic need."

"Doesn't matter why. The act was the same."

"It is very different—look, this is pointless, Theodora. We both know there's much, much more I'm not telling you, so you'll simply have to believe me when I say that I'm not a good man. I must be stopped."

Goddammit! He's so fucking stubborn! Once again, the fact that he felt like he needed to die just to protect everyone from him was yet another testament to his good heart.

"Okay. Fine. You're horrible and evil. You deserve to die, which is why I'm going to kill you.

Just as soon as you tell me about the other times we met—things I said or did or—" I needed more information. Facts.

"There is no time. My brother will be here soon. I can already feel him getting closer."

Dammit. I knew that there was more going on here than just a simple case of me not being able to remember. Something must've happened to make me forget, and it was possible I had the answers to help Mack locked away inside.

"Then just tell me about the last time we met." I was desperate for answers or clues or anything that would tell me what to do.

Mack groaned. Yes, it was a sexy deep groan. *Ignore, ignore, ignore…*

"Please, Mack. Because after you're gone, I will have lost my chance to know." Of course, I had zero intentions of killing this beautiful man.

Mack nodded solemnly and then lifted up his sleeve and pointed to one of the dates written in script on his arm. "This was the last one."

Holy shit. "Those tattoos are a record of us."

"Yes."

Frankly, for such a man to do something so sentimental made my insides liquefy into a sweet syrupy concoction. "That's very…touching."

"It wasn't meant to be. It was the only way I had to mourn my loss."

My brows furrowed. "I didn't realize you took it so hard."

"Every time you died, a piece of me died with you. There's nothing left now."

His words only cemented my resolve. *I'm not throwing in the towel. No fucking way.* My brain barely knew this man, but my heart did. And everything about him made me want to fight tooth and nail to keep him. But if I told him that, the monster would come out.

Out of options, I did the only thing I could that might give him a reason to live. I stood up, pulled my T-shirt over my head, unsnapped my bra, and then slid down my jeans and panties.

Still propped against the couch and sitting on the floor, Mack began grinning with a sweet, almost goofy smile. The kind a guy made when he wanted to get into a little mischief. "Hell. If I'd known showing you a few tattoos would get me into your pants, I would've led with that."

I kneeled down beside him, slid my hands to the back of his neck, and pulled him to my lips. I kissed him with everything I had. "Shut up and fuck me."

Those blue, blue eyes didn't flinch, and those lips didn't stop smiling. "If you insist, but I'm sorry to tell you that I won't be giving you my best work."

I laughed. "What does that mean?"

"I can feel King getting nearer, which means we have less than an hour. To give you a thorough fucking, I need at least six."

Never in a million years would I begin to understand how Mack and King were that connected. It was twin connection unlike anything I'd ever heard of. That said…

"Six hours for sex?" I gulped.

He shrugged. "Fucking is the other thing I'm really good at, but with you, and only you, I like to take my time and savor every second—do it slowly."

"I-I'll take a raincheck on that slow-cook, savoring method."

His expression hardened. "No, Theodora. No more rainchecks. This is the last time."

"Ohmygod. We've done this before, haven't we?"

He nodded. "Yes."

"But you said that your brother always found me first."

"I fucking lied."

"Why, Mack?"

"Because I hate to think about the times when we found each other first and spent the night together. You tried to save me. Something always went wrong. You died. Sometimes while I watched."

Oh crap. How heartbreaking. No wonder he was crazy. I was beginning to think that he wanted to die just so he didn't have to watch me be murdered by King again.

What the *hell* was wrong with his brother?

I offered Mack my most seductive smile, wanting him to forget what we'd just been talking about. "This doesn't mean you changed your mind about the sex, does it?"

He gave me another boyish smile, and I wondered if it was a glimpse of the real him—playful, sweet, carefree.

"Just as long as you promise to keep your word," he said.

Did I really have to lie to this beautiful man?
Whatever it takes.
"Yes. I promise," I fibbed like a common cheat.

He plunged his tongue into my mouth and kissed me with reckless lust. His strong hands cupped my bare breasts, kneading and pinching my hard nipples. I moaned with sinful delight. This was what I wanted. Him. Me. Hard.

I straddled his lap and frantically went to work on his button flies. He lifted his hips so I could slide his jeans down just far enough to spring his thick cock free.

"Wow," was all I could say when I looked at the thing. "That's pretty impressive."

"Wait until you see what it can do," he said with a hint of a proud smile and returned to kissing me.

I slid my hands around his hard flesh, greedily stroking his insane thickness, wanting to work him into a painful frenzy mirroring how my own body felt.

Kissing him wildly, one hand jerking him off, I positioned his soft, velvety head at my wet entrance. All I could think about was getting the length of him inside me. I'd never had sex with a man who was so well endowed, and I'd certainly never slept with one who made me feel like I might combust if I didn't have him immediately.

With his hands gripping my hips, he made a little flexing upward thrust, expediting his penetration.

I threw my head back and gasped, feeling his

large cock push its way, inch by inch, inside me. "Ohgod. You feel so good, Mack."

Meanwhile, he sucked on my nipple, almost to the point of pain, while his soft tongue made sinful little circles around the tip.

I rose up on my knees, relishing the delicious friction of his erection sliding out. He moaned in a deep masculine voice that made me want to hear it again. I slammed down on his dick, the excitement and pleasure of it intermingling with the sounds of our heavy breathing and groans.

"Again," he demanded, his gravelly voice filled with lust.

I slowly rose up again, sliding him out, cupping the back of his silky head of dark hair, kissing him hard. I then brought the weight of my body down on him, the tip of his shaft colliding with the entrance to my womb, sparking a gasp from my mouth and a deep moan from his.

Still deep inside me, he suddenly shifted his legs underneath and brought me down onto my back. He pushed the waistband of his pants down a little further so that I could feel his sack just below my entrance.

"Yes," I moaned. I wanted to feel his muscled back flexing as he drove deep inside me. I wanted to grip that hard ass of his while he pounded his cock into my body. He gave me both.

Pistoning his hips at an eager pace, me raising mine to meet him head-on, grind for grind, I began to climax. I didn't want to. I didn't want to come knowing that we might not get another chance, but my body responded to him at the cellular level. He could've simply breathed into my ear and I would've orgasmed.

Our mouths locked and tongues dancing in a sensual, animalistic rhythm, I rocked my pelvis, and he bore down, grinding his base against my needy, throbbing c-spot.

It was then, of all the blasted moments in the world, that I realized we might have ventured into a world unknown to me, but my body was still a slave to biology. *Fuck. Protection.*

"Mack, I'm going to come," I panted, him riding me hard, kissing me harder.

"Me too," he groaned deliciously.

"I'm not on the pill."

"Neither am I."

Goddammit. I didn't want to stop. Not now, but getting pregnant and...I started coming hard. "OhgodMack. Ohgod." My entire body tensed as I felt a hard, sinful wave of pleasure explode through every nerve ending in my body, blinding my vision with white light. Meanwhile, Mack made short, little jabs with his cock, milking every ounce of pleasure he could from my body.

Now I get it! Now I get it! I screamed in my head, the orgasm filling every corner of my body with sinful contractions laced with ecstasy. Hot baths, long walks, and fake cheese could never compare to this!

It took several delicious moments for me to realize it was over, but then Mack thrust hard with the entire weight of his body and craned his neck toward the ceiling. He then quickly pulled out and gripped his cock in his hand, shooting his cum onto my stomach as I watched. Honestly, it was beyond fucking hot to watch him come.

After a few moments, the hard lust on Mack's face softened, and he lay down at my side, his chest heaving with exertion. "It gets better every time."

God, how I wished I could remember and had all of the missing pieces.

After a few long moments, Mack got a small cloth and cleaned me up. He covered me with a quilted throw that had been hanging on the arm of the couch.

"I'm going to miss this dance, Theodora."

"Dance?"

"Yes. You. Me. The way our bodies move. It's like dancing."

"But without our clothes on."

He chuckled. "Exactly."

"Well, fucking well. What do we have here?" I heard a strange female voice say.

I looked up and there was an anorexic blonde standing over us with a sadistic grin on her familiar face. *The woman from the center?* She was the one who'd come out of Mack's room and dismissed me like a piece of rat trash, which is lower than human trash.

What was she doing here?

Chapter Seventeen

MACK

How the hell did Miranda find us? Yes, I knew she was cunning and had an arsenal of powerful relics that rivaled that of my brother's, but she was the last person I expected to see. Not that I didn't think she'd be looking for me. That was no surprise. I'd only had one chalice but had needed two favors: locating Theodora (to free my soul from the curse) and having the ankh removed (so I couldn't come back to life).

I'd bartered with Miranda to have the ankh removed, and she'd had to call in several other favors from members of the 10 Club to get it done. Talia, another member, helped me find Theodora by loaning me her tracker—a woman with psychic abilities. Yes, Talia owned a woman. Many members of the 10 Club owned people.

And just who was this 10 Club? Take the most powerful, wealthy individuals on earth—oil sheiks, billionaire CEOs, presidents of major countries, and good old-fashioned aristocrats—pluck out all the sadistic fuckers with fetishes, psychotic personalities, and insatiable greed, and put them in a club where they pooled their resources to form alliances that made them impermeable to any law or government. Of course, many of them *are* the government—the Club helped put them there. Membership could get you just about anything, although currency was rarely their currency. Amongst themselves, they bartered for everything from people and weapons to items that fell into more of the occult category. Basically, anything that money couldn't buy.

How did I know so much?

King formed the network thousands of years ago, operating it from behind the scenes, as a means to help him find the Artifact—that stone he needed to come back to life. In the meantime, while he looked, he built his own arsenal and network of power. Of course, now my brother had everything he wanted, including possession of his soul and a body, and he was no longer a sadistic sonofabitch. He was also burdened with trying to figure out how to undo the 10 Club monster he'd created.

I was the cornerstone of his plan.

How?

You guessed it. Killing off the members. No, I didn't feel sorry for them. Those people had plenty of blood on their hands and cared for no one. The previous president, a guy named Vaughn, used to barter for women. Exotic women. He would then charge admission to let people watch him peel the skin from their bodies. Sometimes he took the skins and wrapped them around his dead lover's body so he could play with her. Yes, like I said, they were all sick fuckers. Every last one of them. And I would gladly kill them if it weren't for one simple fact: I needed out. Okay, that and I was just as dangerous as they were. But not as sick. Not even close.

In any case, Miranda was acting president of 10 Club and completely unaware that my brother ran the operations. Most members simply accepted that the person who managed the funds and legalities—including ensuring members never went to prison or were hassled by authorities for their sometimes very illegal activities such as murder, enslavement, and kidnapping—maintained anonymity because he didn't want to become a target. The members were constantly stabbing each other in the back and stealing from one another.

Case in point, I'd given Miranda a fake chalice, and she was now here to collect. With my life.

I sighed. "Miranda, I thought you'd be busy picking fleas from your hair or strangling kittens."

"Mack, who is she?" Theodora asked.

"I'm the bitch who's going to kill him for double-crossing me!" Miranda threw the silver chalice at my head, which I blocked with my hand.

"Where the fuck is the real one, Mack?" Miranda snarled.

"I wish I knew," I lied.

"I'll give you three seconds to give me another answer, or the little bitch loses her head."

I stood from the floor, careful to keep myself positioned between Miranda and Theodora. Life held no value for Miranda, except for the pleasure she derived from taking it. I knew because she used to own me. Almost five long years in her basement. She'd kill me, let me come back, torture me and kill me again. She couldn't get enough. Some days, she'd play out her sexual fantasies before she killed me.

She was evil to the core.

"Well, Miranda, I think we both know how this is going to play out." I was going to do everything in my power to kill her. She would use one of her abilities to subdue me. I would end up dead and she without her answer. Yes, we'd done this dance before when I'd lived in her basement and she wanted information about my brother. But I never talked.

She smiled and flipped her frizzy long blonde hair back over her shoulder. I always wondered why she looked so vile—right down to the animal-print spandex pants and stick figure body. A woman had to work extremely hard to look that bad.

"Yes," she said. "You're going to tell me where the chalice is; then I'm going to slit your throat."

No. What would really happen was she'd try to kill Theodora and me. *Dammit.*

I needed to get Theodora out of here. Of course, that meant Miranda might kill me and my soul would be left wandering the earth, still cursed.

Sonofabitch. Why couldn't I catch a break?

TEDDI

The woman—who I recognized from the mental health center—stood in the doorway of the cabin with her bleach blonde hair teased out into a wild mess of straw, tight pink leopard Spandex pants, and a gold sequin tank top. What struck me as odd, however, was how I felt about her. I wanted to end her life in the most violent of ways.

Why? How the hell should I know! Because, apparently, someone had done a number on me and made me forget my past. Only, some part of me remembered the emotional impressions I had of people. I loved Mack. I was afraid of King. And I hated this bitch. Seriously fucking hated her.

"Love the outfit, lady. Hope you win," I said.

She gave me a look and then brought her attention back to Mack. "Who's the little slut, Mack?"

Mack slid on his jeans, completely unashamed of letting this woman see him naked and looking cool as ice. "Someone I picked up to pass the time."

"Bullshit," she replied. "I'm getting a vibe off of her. What's she do?"

Mack shook his head. "She's not for sale, Miranda."

Sale. What the fuck?

She shrugged. "Fine. Then maybe I'll just take her."

Mack growled. "How about this? I'll tell you

where the real chalice is if you let her leave."

"Do I still get to kill you?" Miranda asked.

"Sure," he replied.

"Mack, no!" I protested. What was he doing? Because according to him, I was the only one who could end his life. Meaning, if this woman did it, he'd end up some tormented, disembodied cursed soul again.

Mack glanced over his shoulder at me. "Go. I'll be fine. Miranda is within her rights since I conned her."

"I'm not leaving, Mack." In fact, my brain had already located a weapon and had figured out a plan of attack. There was a small knife on the counter next to my car keys. I would grab them both, slide by this woman and take her out.

Jesus. Who the hell am I? Because apparently, I was no stranger to killing. Double-O-Teddi.

"I'm not asking," Mack said.

I dropped the blanket I'd been holding around my naked body and then threw on my dark sweater and jeans, acting severely pissy about it. I walked over to the small counter, angling my body so that the woman wouldn't see my move. I gripped the knife in my right hand with my keys, holding the blade pressed flat along the inside of my wrist to conceal it as best as possible. "Mack, I really think you should—"

"Just go!" he yelled.

"Fine. I got what I wanted anyway." I shot him one last look for effect and slid past him. The woman was just to the right of the door and only a few feet away. She wasn't threatened by me because she didn't move an inch as I approached.

Lucky me.

Right as I got to her side, I made my move, swiping sideways for her neck. But faster than my eye could register, she moved out of the way just as Mack lunged. The knife hit Mack right in his neck.

I screamed.

CHAPTER EIGHTEEN

TEDDI

The blonde woman laughed hysterically as Mack stumbled and fell over, cupping his hand over the wound. The blood didn't just dribble, it flowed like an open spigot.

"Mack!" I dropped the knife and jumped to his side, kneeling beside him. "Oh, God. What did I do?"

"I bet right about now, he's wishing he hadn't taken off that necklace," the woman chuckled out her words. I ignored her. All I could see were colors all around Mack, black and blues, and they were fading fast. "No, no, no." I pushed my hands over his jugular, but it was no use.

Mack just lay there, his blue, blue eyes staring at the ceiling. "It's finally happening," he whispered. "You kept your promise. Thank you."

"No. I was lying! I'm not ready to let you go!" I said. "I can change things for you." If I'd just had more time.

"I'm not worth helping, Theodora. But I love you. I always have and I always will." He gasped for air. "Tell King..." His voice dropped so low I could barely hear him. It sounded like he'd said he wanted to be warm or put somewhere warm or…

Fuck! This can't be happening! "I love you, too! I love you, too! Don't go." The life faded from his eyes right before mine. "No. No. No, Mack," I yelled. "I won't let you leave me." But he was already gone. Just like that. And I felt a part of my soul go with him. How could this have happened? How could I have done this horrible thing to this beautiful man just as King said I would?

I sobbed over his body, wishing I could somehow turn back the clock or use these "gifts" I supposedly had.

"What a shithead," the woman behind me said. "Now I'm going to have to find the chalice the hard way. As for you, little girl, I don't take kindly to attempts on my life."

I grabbed the knife from the floor beside me and, in one fluid motion, threw it at her. The tip lodged into her right eye, and she dropped to the floor like a bag of wet sand. Where and how had I come up with such a skill? I didn't know and I didn't care.

I turned back to Mack and watched in despair as his features faded back to the man I'd first met—dirty blond hair, light golden skin, honey brown stubble. Meaning, the Mack I'd first met, the man I'd fallen in love with so long ago, his soul was gone from this body.

"No," I heard a deep voice gasp from the

doorway. I glanced over my shoulder, and King just stood there staring at his dead brother in disbelief. Mia instantly had tears falling down her cheeks.

"You fucking bitch!" King roared at me. "I should've killed you when I had the chance." He stepped toward me, but Mia pulled him back.

"King, no."

He turned his rage toward her, shaking his finger in her face. "This is your fault. I shouldn't have listened to you."

I saw the wounded look in her eyes.

"It was an accident," I muttered, wiping away the stream of tears in my eyes. "I was taking a swipe at that woman, but Mack rushed in and..." I couldn't finish my words.

"Do you really think it fucking matters?" King growled, looking like a savage predator despite his finely tailored black suit. "I can't bring him back this time!"

He began reaching for me, and once again Mia interceded. "You can't kill her, King. Mack wouldn't have wanted it and neither do I."

He looked at her, and all I could see was a red light glowing all around him. Rage, I thought. It was the color of rage.

"Just..." Mia blew out a breath. "Just take a minute outside, King. Please."

He shook his head from side to side, a look of sheer madness in his eyes. It broke my heart to see him in so much pain for something I'd done, but it broke my heart more to see the lifeless body stretched out in front of me.

"Mack, I don't know if you can hear me, but I'm begging; please don't leave." Yes, I was speaking to his spirit. No, I knew nothing about how it all worked, but I hoped that he would choose not to go wherever souls went after they were freed from obscenely unjust and torturous three-thousand-year-old curses.

I felt Mia's warm hand on my shoulder as she kneeled down next to me.

"It all just happened so fast," I said, sobbing quietly. "I was trying to save him. I really was."

"I know, sweetie."

She took Mack's hand and held it between hers, closing her eyes as if praying. After a few moments, she reopened her big blues. "I can't feel any connection to him." She sounded very worried.

"What does that mean?" I asked.

She looked down at his beautiful, lifeless face. "That the chances of getting him back are not good. Once the soul's moved on, it's like trying to capture water with a sieve."

"Oh God, no."

"That's why King has been looking for that Incan chalice—it can resurrect anyone, even if the soul has moved on."

I looked at her through my blurry teary eyes. "You *were* looking for it." Mack had mentioned that he'd stolen something from them and that was the reason "they" were trying to find him.

"King was looking for it and Mack was helping him. I lost my brother last year and hoped to get him back, but now I wonder if it just wasn't meant to be. He had issues. But Mack…" She sighed and ran her hand down the side of his cheek, staring lovingly at his pale face. "Mack saved my life. He helped King find himself again, and as much as I love my brother, Mack risked a lot to help us. I just don't know what we'll do without him."

It was all too fresh in my mind and heart. Hell, the body was still warm.

"Aren't you a Seer?" I asked. "Don't you have powers or something? You can bring him back!"

She shook her head. "I gave up my gifts to be with King—a long story, but everything in our world requires a sacrifice. A counterbalance or a trade-off. I traded my abilities for the thing I loved most." She looked at me with pity. "Our only chance is finding that chalice."

"How the hell do we do that?" I asked.

She glanced toward the open door leading outside. "I married the man who can find anything."

"If it's that easy to find the chalice, then why hasn't he?"

She gave me a look. "Who said anything about easy? It took the man over three thousand years to find the rock I used to bind his curse." Someday I'd have to ask her how she happened to be alive. From what I deduced, she knew King and Mack three thousand years ago. But that just didn't matter right now.

I can't accept this. I can't, I thought, looking at Mack's beautiful face.

"We'll do everything we can to find the chalice. I promise," Mia said.

"What about your brother?"

She looked down at the lifeless hand cupped between hers. "Mack once gave me the choice between bringing back King or my brother. It was the hardest decision I've ever made because I knew how losing Justin destroyed my parents, but I made my choice that day. I chose King. I will always choose him until my last breath. I choose him now. And that man doesn't know how to live or breathe without his twin—the connection they have is too deep." She sighed. "Saving Mack is saving the man I love."

"I love you, Mia," said a deep, gravelly voice from behind us.

We both swiveled our heads toward King, who stood in the doorway, his fit arms stretching the black fabric of his finely tailored suit. And I had to admit, it wasn't easy looking at the spitting image of the man I'd just made love to less than a handful of minutes ago. My heart ached for him in a way I'd never be able to articulate.

Mia stood and walked over to King, pushing herself onto her tiptoes to reach his lips. I felt so envious of the two. Come what may, they had each other.

Me?

I had a past I couldn't remember and my heart lying bled out on the floor in front of me. I didn't know the man, yet he was everything to me.

"How much?" I said.

I didn't hear a reply, so I glanced at King and Mia. They looked confused.

I repeated, "How much? How fucking much to bring him back?"

King frowned at me, clearly insulted. "You think I'd accept money for something like that?"

I shrugged. "All I know about you is that you've murdered me without mercy. And according to your wife here, you're the guy who can find anything."

He shook his head. "I wouldn't even wipe my ass for you."

"King," Mia scolded.

"No." He shot her a stern look. "There's a reason I've kept killing her, and it's lying on the floor right now. She can burn in hell."

"I just want Mack back. That's all," I argued.

"You can find a deep dark hole to wither and die in. *I* will get my brother back."

"I am not going to sit on my ass, waiting and hoping," I said. "Not when he's just as important to me as he is to you."

King had a sinister look in his eyes.

"King, no," Mia protested. "I know what you're thinking. But your bartering days are over."

Okay. What *was* King thinking? I continued listening.

"Not exactly," King admitted.

"What?" Mia snapped. "But you told me you were done with running the 10 Club."

Later, I would learn what the 10 Club was and why Mia seemed so adamant about King not being a part of it. For the moment, however, it was just one more piece of a world I was only beginning to understand.

"Mack was helping me dismantle it," King said. "Obviously, that's now put on hold. And I cannot leave it to run itself or someone else will take power. I must remain in charge until I can figure out a new plan."

"Fuckingshit, King. No," she barked. "Those people are dangerous."

"So am I," he replied.

"We have a baby. We have a life now," she pleaded.

"Which is why you will return to the safety of our home in Crete while I do what I must to locate the chalice and take care of this hiccup with the 10 Club leadership." He turned and looked at me. "As for you, I meant what I said. And I will give you five seconds to leave this place before I kill you for the sixth time. Or is it the seventh? I cannot remember."

Mia's face turned an angry shade of red. "I won't let you—"

"No," I interrupted. "It's fine. I'll go if it means I get to see Mack again."

King growled. "If you so much as breathe my brother's name again, I will remove your head and place it in a jar. But you won't die, little Seer. You'll live—for thousands of years if I wish it—screaming for help. But no one will hear you. Not a soul." Mia opened her mouth to speak as he turned toward her. "And before you say a word, woman, I will remind you what you did to the man who gutted your brother like a fish."

Mia snapped her mouth shut and looked up at

him, visibly fuming. Yes, I now wanted to know what happened to this man King had just spoken of, but I had bigger issues, and clearly it was pretty heinous if it could make this Mia woman stop talking. Still, I had to plead my case. I had to try.

"I don't care if I ever see Mack again," I lied. "I just want to get him back. I want to know that he's all right. Please, just let me help."

I guessed that King didn't like that idea, because I felt something slam my body into the wall before I blacked out.

⁂

When I woke, still in that cabin, I felt like I had been dismembered by a taffy puller. Every fiber of my being ached and felt paper thin, unable to carry its own weight. I glanced over to the spot where Mack's body had been.

Gone. So was the woman.

I groaned and rolled from my side onto my back, wishing I was dead, too. I missed Mack. I missed him so much that all I could think of was digging that hole King had mentioned.

Mack. Mack. Less than a week ago I had been a woman focused on her career. I'd lived a life that was colorless and absent of love. Now, I loved so much that I could hardly breathe. Yes, I barely knew this man. But my heart and soul knew him like the sound of my own voice. It was such a difficult thing to have such a profound connection with a person and not have the memories of how you got there—dates, a first kiss, making love for the first time.

And as I lay there, wheezing and trying to find the strength to get up and fight, one question circulated in my mind.

Why can't I remember?

It seemed that my memories wanted to push through but couldn't. Whoever had done this to me didn't want me to learn about my past with Mack or find him. And I didn't get the impression that King (or Mia) had anything to do with it.

So why? What was it they wanted to hide from me?

I started to sob, dripping with misery, drenched in agony. *Fight, Óolal. Fight. That bastard King can't really hurt you, and he knows it.* It was that voice inside me speaking. Me. Not me. Familiar and unfamiliar.

"How can I fight when I can't even move?" I whispered.

Without reason or thought on the matter, I painfully edged my hands over my heart. I closed my eyes and stopped fighting the pain. Something inside told me to let it in.

I inhaled the hurt and consumed its heavy weight, like eating cement. Within seconds, I felt myself fading away to another place…

※

I am standing at the edge of a giant ballroom with white walls and gold trim, watching the other extravagantly dressed guests bow and twirl to the orchestra. I can't believe I am here at yet another ball. I'm too old for this and have no desire to marry. At least not any man I've ever met. They all smell like perfumed poodles or speak only of my dowry. My friend and companion Lucida, on the other hand, lives for the day she is wed. Of course, she is proper wife material. I am not. I read incessantly—science, philosophy, religion, and politics. I argue with my father. I refuse to do as I am told. My heart is wild and untamable and always will be.

I glance over at the grandfather clock in the corner of the massive room crowded with people who are laughing and drinking and judging one and other. One more hour of this horseshit and I am free to go. My older cousin Robert will chaperone me, as my father is away on business and my mother is feeling a bit "under the weather." Really, she loathes these social events as much as I do, but this is my last season before I will officially be declared a spinster. *I cannot wait.* There is great freedom in being an old maid—no husband to make demands, no children to discipline, no more balls to attend.

As I try not to fidget or tug at my cream-colored silk dress to relieve the pressure of the whalebone digging into my rib cage, I feel someone watching me from across the room.

Oh, glorious. Yet another man I will have to politely shoo away with an excuse about my worn-out feet. But when I look up, a stunning pair of blue, blue eyes meet mine, and I feel like the wind has been sucked from my lungs. I start to fall backward, unable to keep myself upright.

"Madam, are you unwell?" says a man to my side who had been chatting with my friend Lucinda about something trivial related to gardens.

I find my legs again and nod. "Yes, I am fine. My dress is a little tight."

Lucinda, who is a petite-framed thing with golden locks—the exact opposite of me with my black hair and dark eyes—lets out a little laugh. "Evelyn, you really will go to any length to leave early. But I'm not having it. You made a promise to stay to the last dance."

This is the point where I would normally begin begging her to leave, appealing to her love for me, as we've been lifelong friends, but this time I do not wish to go anywhere. At least, not with her.

I watch the stranger approach, weaving between an ocean of billowing ruffled skirts and men in black coats. He is a head taller than the rest and a thousand times more beautiful than any man I've ever laid eyes upon—shoulder-length sandy-blond hair, wide shoulders, and a pronounced jawline. The way he walks, with such confidence and ease, gives him an air of power. Or danger. I am unsure. Whatever the case, I cannot take my eyes away, and he cannot seem to remove his gaze from me.

I have seen him before. I know I have. Yet I cannot recall ever meeting him, and this was the sort of man no woman could ever forget.

The man finally reaches me and stares down, holding me in place with those stunning azure eyes.

"It's you, isn't it?" he says in a voice so deep and masculine that my toes curl inside my silk slippers underneath my gown.

Dear Lord, no. He thinks I am someone else. My heart is broken. Right then and there.

"You have mistaken me, sir, for someone else," I say acerbically. It's just my luck that this man, this beautiful, wild-looking man who clearly doesn't belong at a ball, though his clothes appear fine enough, would be in search of another woman.

He holds out his hand, a very improper gesture, as we have not been introduced. "I never make mistakes."

I glance at his awaiting hand and cannot help wanting it. He's simply too magnificent to deny.

I reach for him, and the moment I do, images flash through my mind. I see myself and him together, though he looks different. His features are dark and the planes of his face are exquisitely sculpted like a marble statue of a Greek god. But nevertheless, I know those eyes and their endless blues. And I know how he feels when he holds me and kisses me.

"Who are you?" I whisper.

"They call me Macarius." His eyes shift around the room as if checking for someone. "Come, we must leave quickly."

Lucinda is now dancing and paying me no attention. My cousin Robert is occupied with a young blonde in the corner, surely attempting to convince her to meet somewhere later so he can rob her of her virtue.

"Where will we go?" I ask, knowing it doesn't matter.

Macarius smiles, but I can see it isn't genuine. There's a certain darkness in his lovely light eyes. He is dangerous. I want to be with him anyway.

He pulls me by the hand out the side door leading to a large fountain situated beside a long, torch-lit garden. The other guests will likely assume we are going to do something scandalous behind one of the many large trees, and I know my reputation will be soiled. I don't care. I follow Macarius, and we silently make our way through the grounds, out a side gate, onto the street. The sound of horse hooves clicking, pulling carriages, fills the chilly air.

As we walk in silence, my gloved hand in his, more images come crashing down on me. Jungle, rain, a small dwelling. I see this man over me, sliding his naked body between my thighs, breathing into my hair.

Dear God. What is happening? Still, I am unafraid. I want only to be with him. I am burning for him.

We turn the corner and enter the front gate of a large white house with pillars in the front. I know this home. I've seen it a million times. It was once owned by the governor, but he departed from San Francisco months ago. Rumor has it that a wealthy merchant from New York has purchased the estate but has not yet taken up residence. Obviously, they were mistaken. Here he is.

And he's all mine.

We enter through the front door into a lavish foyer of white marble and muraled ceilings. Every thought running through my head tells me that my parents will disown me when word gets out that I am here. Yes, the servants will talk. They always do.

We go into his sitting room, where a fire is already lit. Cognac is set out on a small table beside the pastel blue couch.

"So this is your home? It's lovely," I say.

Macarius releases my hand and goes to pour himself a tall glass. "Care for a drink?" he asks, ignoring my comment.

"No. Thank you. I do not drink spirits. But can you…" I can't seem to find the words I want to say. *What in God's name is happening to me?*

He guzzles his drink and sets down his glass, staring into the fire. "Do you have any idea how long I have been looking for you?"

"How can this be if we've only just met?"

He turns and looks at me sternly with those deep blue eyes. "You and I both know that's not true, Óolal."

"My name is Evelyn. Evelyn Burgess."

"Call yourself whatever name pleases you. It does not change the fact that you are mine and that I am taking you up to my chamber."

I am too stunned to move. I have never been with anyone.

"Why do I have memories of you?" I finally ask.

He steps towards me and places his hands on my shoulders. "Because you and I are connected. Until our last breaths, in this life and the next." He bends slowly and presses his lips to mine. More memories flood in. I see faces of people with dark skin and black hair gathered around a fire. I think I loved them once, but they made me very unhappy. They wouldn't let me love someone.

"I do not understand," I say, pulling away.

"You don't have to. Simply listen to your heart."

Once again he takes my hand and leads me up a long marble staircase into his bedchamber where another warm fire fights the chill of the winter night outside. If there are servants in this home, I haven't seen one yet, and for this I feel relieved.

He closes the door and locks it behind us. And somewhere, a part of my brain is telling me this is madness to walk out of a ball with a man I have never met, to go to his home unaccompanied, to give myself to him. Yet the other part of my mind tells me that I have been waiting for this my entire life.

He rushes to me and kisses me hard, his strong hands cupping the back of my head to bring me closer. His lips are soft, and he tastes like liquor. His wickedly skilled tongue slides against mine, and he enters my mouth, exploring and tasting me, breathing into me.

Before I know what's happening, he pushes me back onto his large four-post bed, lifting up my skirts.

"I'm sorry, but I cannot wait." He lies over me, and I see his hand moving to unbutton the front of his black breeches.

I can barely stand the anticipation, and when his warm strong hands find my wet and ready entrance, he wastes little time to position his cock.

I hold my breath and wait for him to enter. I've heard so many unpleasant things about what it feels like to lie with a man, but now my memories are urging me to do this. I know how good he will make me feel.

"I love you. You know that, don't you?" he says as he stares into my eyes. I suddenly see colors bursting all around him. Yellows and whites veined with black and red.

I can't speak as he drives into me, pushing through the barrier with his large cock. It feels like I might break, but as he slides in deeper and stops, the sting begins to subside.

I release my breath, knowing the worst is over.

"Ready for more?" he says in that deep hypnotic voice.

"Yes. More."

He pulls out and drives in again. This time it feels good. So, so good. I raise my hips to get more of him.

As he begins pumping into me, he works my breasts free from the top of my dress and bends his body to take my nipple in his mouth. The sensation sparks a delicious contraction deep in my belly.

Oh, God. Where has this man been all my life? I throw my head back, moaning in ecstasy. I know that from this moment on, there will never be another.

Macarius's pace begins to quicken, and he

returns to my lips, kissing me deeply, panting in time to my own quick breaths. We touch, we pant, we move like hungry animals, and all the while I see more images of him and me. We are in different places and times, yet he always looks at me the same way. So much love and sorrow in those eyes.

Before I realize it, the sweet, sweet pressure builds and then…I explode. My body lights up with sinful contractions as he presses the weight of his long frame into my juncture, spilling his warm seed inside me. I grab fistfuls of soft sheets as the wave of pleasure racks my body until I'm left a quivering heap.

He collapses on top of me, and I can hardly breathe, but I don't care. Feeling him inside me, our bodies together, is like no other sensation I've ever experienced.

"God, I missed you," he whispers into my hair. "I can't believe I found you."

"You came to the ball looking for me?" I murmur.

"No. I was there to kill a woman. A very bad woman who murdered her husband for his fortune. I was taking my leave when I spotted you across the room."

I freeze in shock.

"What? Have you forgotten that part, too?" he asks.

I blink up at the white ceiling dancing with licks of orange from the fireplace. "Yes."

He sighs and withdraws, rolling over onto his back beside me. "Well, let me remind you, then. I was cursed by your father, who killed you because we made love and he believed it would displease the gods. He sentenced me to an eternity of reliving his torment. Giving in to the curse—killing—is the only thing that provides me a moment of peace from the darkness gnawing at my soul."

As Macarius speaks, my own mind shows me the horrific memories. It is frightening and amazing all at once.

He continues, "But we were in love, so before you died, you used your gifts to bind your soul to mine. You said that you would find me and free me."

Gifts. Yes, I have gifts. I can heal broken bones and take away sickness. My people thought I was some manner of demigod.

I sit up and gasp. "I remember now. I remember everything."

"Good. Because I need you to free me from this curse, Evelyn. I cannot stand it any longer."

Oh Lord. It all hits me in one fell swoop. The suffering he has endured over thousands of years, my search for him over many lifetimes.

"I am not sure I know how." I only recall that moment of my death and wanting to save him with all my soul.

He grabs me and pulls me down to his lips. "You simply need a little more reminding." He kisses me again, and I feel my body giving in to my need for him. We spend the night making up for lost time, and I can only think of how happy I am. I must find a way to save this beautiful man.

At first light, I dress and slip out of his home while he remains asleep, a vision of male perfection. It is a long walk back to my house on the other side of town, but I am fortunate enough to see a cab passing. The driver takes one look at me and shakes his head. He thinks I'm a whore of some sort, but money is money, so he brings me home.

I slip in through the servants' entrance in the back of our respectable Victorian-style house, ignoring the whispers and giggles of the staff. I couldn't care less.

"Tell the footman to ready the carriage," I bark out in a hurry.

Our maid, Bessy, gives me a look, and I know what she is thinking. It's early in the morning, and I have no chaperone. I am up to no good.

She's right.

I go up to my room, throw on my daily outing dress—blue with white trim—my heavy black wool coat, and a black hat. I don't want to be noticed on the street.

I grab the bit of gold coins I have hidden underneath my chest of drawers, knowing that what I am about to do is insane. I am about to make a deal with the devil, but there is nothing I won't do to save Macarius.

I rush out of the house and into the awaiting carriage. I slide open the little window to speak to my driver. "Take me to the dark house."

Everyone who lives in San Francisco knows this home that sits high on a hill overlooking the mouth of the bay, constantly covered in a sheet of fog no matter the time of year. The servants believe it is haunted by a ghost. The local merchants say that the man who lives there is mad, but pays a fair price for anything they procure for him. The gentlemen of society say that this man is dangerous, but that he can find anything or anyone. For a price.

The carriage stops in front of the three-story house with dark blue paint and large white shutters. The unkempt front yard, full of leaves and overgrown vegetation poking through the wrought-iron gate, gives the place a foreboding look. But now I know who and what I am. I remember everything. This place is full of power. And if anyone can help me find what I am searching for, it is him.

I tell the driver to wait and let myself inside the gate. As I get closer to the multicolored stained-glass door, goose bumps explode all over my body. The air is filled with energy. Bad energy. I can actually see it seeping from the ground and the woodwork.

I knock, but no one answers. *Lord. He has to be in there.* I can feel him watching me, reading me. Finally, the door pops and swings open with a loud creak.

"Hello?" It's dark inside, and I can see colors—imprints, if you will—of those who've entered before me. Some have met their fates in this house. I might meet mine, too. But helping Macarius is all that matters.

I enter the dark foyer, sensing that something is near.

"Come into the sitting room," says an ominous voice that suddenly makes me wish I hadn't come.

I cautiously enter and see the dark form of a man sitting in the corner. He's barely visible to me.

"What do you want, woman?"

I clear my throat. "Sir, I am told that you locate objects for people."

"And what is it you wish to locate? A husband? A lost slipper?" There's amusement in his tone, but I ignore it.

"I wish to break a curse. I have gold if you wish to see it."

"What kind of curse?" he says, his interest sounding piqued.

"The kind that was made by an angry father."

The man chuckles under his breath, and it sends sharp painful tingles down my spine. "Let me guess. This father is displeased by your romantic choices."

I nod. "More or less."

"Well, you best be on your way, little girl. I do not find that which has been lost up one's asshole such as your father's patience. But I assure you, his disapproval is not a curse; it is merely an inconvenience. Please show yourself out."

How dare he. "I am not some naïve little girl seeking a charm to gain my father's approval. And if you are as powerful as everyone says, you would know that."

I'm wasting my time here, and I turn to leave, wondering how I'll ever fix the man I care for more than life itself.

"Wait," the man says as I step toward the front

door. "Come back here."

I return to the room, where he's no longer sitting in the shadows but is standing in the soft light filtering through a gap in the drawn curtains.

Good Lord. I know him. He looks like Macarius once did. More memories pop into my head—of this man hunting me down with his sword, of me begging for my life. I realize this man is his twin brother. He is vicious and cruel. He has no light inside him despite his utter masculine beauty and fine clothes.

This is some sick turn of fate.

And he is a ghost, I realize. A soul who out of sheer spite for this world has refused to go. He clings to this world so fiercely, he appears real to the naked eye. To my eyes, however, I see right through him. Literally and figuratively.

I instinctively shut it all out. I've made a grave mistake coming here. *Oh God, this man will kill me if he realizes who I am.*

"I, uhhh...I have changed my mind." I turn to leave.

"How unfortunate," he says, "because I have the answer to your question."

I stop just short of the front door, feeling torn between saving myself and saving Macarius. Logic would tell me that his own brother would have helped him by now if he'd had the means. *Unless...I am the key as Macarius says.*

I turn and face the towering figure who is a mere five feet away. I know it's only a question of moments before he recognizes me.

"What's the price?" I ask, trying not to sound nervous.

"This one is on the house, because you will find the answer very disagreeable."

I am not encouraged by this, as to be expected.

He continues, "Death is the only way to truly end a curse such as that."

"And if the soul has been cursed?"

"Then the soul must die, too—it must move on from this world, detach from anything that doesn't truly belong to it. But you know that already, don't you, Óolal?"

Balls. He knows.

Before another word leaves my mouth, the man evaporates right before my eyes and reappears behind me, snapping my neck. And all I can think of in that split second is that I didn't kiss Macarius goodbye.

Will I see him again in my next life?

മ

"Fuck!" I sat up, clawing at my neck, realizing that I was back in that strange cabin in the desert.

It's just a dream. Just a dream. But goddammit, it wasn't. I was there, in the moment, living every breath and emotion. Each second had felt just as real as the throbbing in my skull.

I grabbed the sides of my head, grasping how the rest of my body felt. Perfect. I ran my hands over my torso. *Whatthehell?*

While I'd been away, I had healed.

I can heal! That was what I had said during my "dream."

Slowly, I got to my feet, noticing the pools of sticky-looking blood on the floor where Mack's and that woman's body had been. King and Mia had taken them. To where? Who knew? All that mattered was Mack was dead and I killed him. Killed him. Yes, it was an accident, but that didn't make it any less painful or horrific. To add frosting on my shitty cake, I then killed a second person. I'd had cause, but once again, what did it matter? Two deaths by my hand. Me. Theodora Valentine.

But you're going to fix this. At least, I'd fix one of the deaths. I wasn't ready to let Mack go three thousand years ago, and I wasn't ready to let him go now.

So how would I get him back? That chalice seemed like my only hope. Of course, King was already looking for it, and I had no doubt he would find it. But here was the thing: Mack was dead, and if his soul had crossed over to this other side King mentioned, Mack was now free from my father's poison. However, if King brought him back, Mack would still be tormented. That had been Mack's point all along. He didn't want to live with the pain and guilt of his memories.

But I can heal him. It was my gift. It always had been. Now I just needed to convince that dark, evil sonofabitch King that just bringing Mack back wasn't enough. He needed *me*.

Chapter Nineteen

San Francisco. 8:45 p.m.

With very little effort, I found that foggy hill overlooking the Golden Gate from my dreams. And though the old dark house had been leveled long ago—a crisp-white, modern-day palace with floor-to-ceiling windows sitting in its place—it was that same dreary old home with that ominous vibe.

I entered the meticulously landscaped yard filled with vibrant flowers—violets, reds, and yellows—and approached the all-glass front door with a view of the tiled foyer and potted palms.

I reached out my hand to push the doorbell, but then thought to myself how formality and politeness were a waste of time. King had taken my life multiple times. Once in this very spot. That made us like family, right? A really, really dysfunctional family, of course.

I clamped down the lever on the door handle and pushed, not at all surprised to find it unlocked. A cocky sonofabitch like King would never bolt his front door because he'd kill anyone who had the gall to intrude. Which was why I half expected him to come rushing toward me with a giant spear or cleaver or something sharp.

Instead, I heard music, voices, and laughter coming from a room just off of the foyer.

A party?

I hit pause for a moment, thinking this through. My goal was to persuade King to not kill me and to let me help him get his brother's life back. Would crashing his dinner party help or hinder?

Help. He might behave more rationally if there were people around he wanted to impress. So that was that; I marched down the short hall and stopped in the doorway of the tennis-court-sized living room. *Jeez. Big enough?* Although most of the people inside, wearing tuxes and evening gowns, were crowded around the bar at the far end of the room or were pouring out through two French doors onto a patio.

There had to be at least a hundred people inside.

"What the hell are you doing here, little Seer?" said a deep, menacing voice.

I turned and looked up at the very unhappy man with the misleadingly handsome face and dark hair combed back to give him a sophisticated look. It hurt to look at King. It really did. Because all I could see was Mack.

I cleared my throat. "So. A party, huh?"

He immediately got the undertone of my criticism. His brother hadn't even been dead twenty-four hours, and he was throwing a soiree.

"I should've broken your neck," he growled.

"Why didn't you?"

"I promised Mia that if you stayed away, I would let you live. I'd like to thank you for not staying away. Shall I kill you now, or would you like a drink first?"

"How gracious."

He dipped his silky head of black hair, and I resisted the urge to run my fingers through its thickness, pretending it was Mack.

"It's the least I can do since you've granted my wish," he replied.

Yeah. Just try to kill me. I fucking dare you, I thought. But instead, I said, "I'm a bit underdressed for your party. Why don't we go somewhere private? There's something I need to discuss with you—a proposition I want to make—before you kill me, of course."

"I'm afraid I can't leave my own event—too many wolves to watch," he said in a low voice.

I looked around the room, and that was when I noticed it. The colors. Everyone here oozed reds and black. I didn't really know what the colors meant specifically, other than they were not good.

"Crap." There was so much evil in this room, it nearly sent me to my knees.

"Crap indeed," said King.

The small quartet in the corner of the room ended the current ballad and started playing a light jazzy tune. I didn't know the song, but it was lively and joyful, despite being slow. The polar opposite of the guests in the room.

King held out his hand. "Shall we dance?"

"Dance? With you?"

"Yes. The people here are very dangerous and not without their own gifts. I'm guessing there are at least five who've already realized you're not simply a regular person. And unfortunately for you, Miss Valentine, you are unclaimed property."

"That's Dr. Valentine, and I am no one's property."

He laughed and dropped his hand. "Suit yourself, but you're in our world now. And here, if you don't belong to someone, you're fair game."

Disgusting. "Fine. If dancing with you will give me time to say my piece, then let's do it."

He dipped his head in a suave, gentlemanly way and then held out his hand and led me to the corner of the room where the band played. We faced each other and locked hands. The man was definitely at ease in his own skin, because he moved like smooth butter sliding down warm bread. Effortless.

"Nice moves," I said with a hint of disdain.

"Thank you. Now, what is this proposal of yours, little Seer?"

I tightened my grip on his warm hand, wishing I could cause him a little pain. But even his palms felt powerful.

"Do you know what my gift is, King?"

"Yes. It's annoying the hell out of me and killing my only living blood."

I shook my head. *Asshole.* "I am a healer."

There was a moment when he broke his icy

façade. He was surprised.

"You didn't know that, did you?" I asked.

"What is your point?" he said, not answering my question.

"That you're focusing on saving Mack's physical form. But not his soul. He's tormented, King. He wanted to die. He practically begged me to end his suffering because he can't live with all of the things he's done over his lifetime. And if you don't believe me, then ask yourself why he had that necklace removed."

King blinked and glanced over my shoulders. Ever the watchful eye.

"You can relate, can't you?" I asked, but it wasn't a question. "You were cursed, too. You probably have nightmares about all of the horrible things you've done."

Hell, they coined the phrase "Draconian" in his honor.

"Again, little Seer, I ask you your point."

"I can heal Mack. I can take away his pain so that when you bring him back, he won't just be alive, he'll be happy."

He scoffed. "I think you're exaggerating your gifts so that I won't kill you."

"I think you're just looking for any excuse to kill me."

"Perhaps," he conceded.

Okay then. Could I prove it to him? In all honesty, I didn't know how to use my gift, but I had to try.

I closed my eyes for a moment, swaying to the

music, reaching with my mind somewhere inside me.

Nothing happened.

Try again. Try again. Mack was counting on me.

Then an image of Mack flashed in my head, and I began to feel the warm glow of white light swirling in a tightly packed ball. Was this what healed people? It had to be.

I struggled and pushed, thinking of Mack, visualizing that ball of light traveling down one arm and flowing through my hand, through the barrier of my skin, and absorbing into King's hand. He suddenly froze and then so did I. I felt this strange rush of something going through me and into him, our souls connected. I wasn't just healing him, I was acting as a conduit of sorts, transferring this…whatever it was…into him. Where the white healing light came from, I could only guess, but as I drew from it, I realized it wasn't inside me. It was…well, crap. I didn't know. On some other plane of existence, I guessed.

Several more moments passed, and then our connection was broken by someone tapping King on the shoulder.

We both pulled away from each other, shocked and mildly disoriented.

King and I swiveled our heads to find a medium height man in a tux, with brown hair and a small scar on his right cheek.

"May I cut in?" he asked with a wolfish smile.

King looked at me, looked at the man, and then looked at me again. He then did something extremely disturbing: He slid his hands around my waist and pulled me into his tall frame, almost protectively.

"The woman is mine," he growled. "So fuck the hell off."

The man's smile dropped, and I saw a look of evil hate in his eyes. "Very well. How much do you want for her?"

"She's not for sale."

King was protecting me? Holy cow.

He went on, "I'm saving her for another trade. You don't have anything I want." King's icy blue eyes flickered with a menacing vibe.

What in the world? These people were really fucked up.

The man dipped his head. "We'll see about that."

King's eyes were glued to the back of the man's head like a vicious watchdog until he disappeared outside into the crowd.

"What was that?" I asked.

King snapped out of whatever zone he'd been in and looked at me. "You're not safe here."

I laughed. "And you care?"

He stared at me with those sky blue eyes, the planes of his handsome face filled with an unreadable distress. "Yes. I do. And if you ever tell anyone, I will deny it."

"So it worked," I muttered to myself, completely astonished.

King frowned, grabbed my hand, and dragged me from the room.

"Where are you taking me?"

"To my bedroom to *fuck!*" he said, nice and loud.

What the... I tried to pull my hand away, which only provoked a sharper reaction: him throwing me over his shoulder and marching upstairs. Meanwhile the room of guests fell into a swarming sound of whispers, gasps, and laughter. At our expense, obviously.

Ohmygod. Ohmygod. What is happening? I had to think fast. Clearly King had lost his goddamned mind! Something must've gone wrong when I used my gift!

We entered a room, and he slammed a set of double doors shut, locked them, and then tossed me down onto a large bed.

"What are you doing!" I yelled.

"What the fuck do you think?" he yelled back and then leaned in, placing his index finger to his mouth to shush me.

Screw that! I lunged off the bed to the side and tried to skirt around him. Faster than my eyes could register, he caught me and threw me back down again.

"Woman," he hissed, "calm the fuck down. They need to believe you are mine. Understand?"

Lightbulb. "So you're not going to rape me?"

He frowned, blatantly offended by the notion, which only amplified my relief.

"Do not let the tuxes fool you. These people are animals, Theodora. They only understand cruelty and barbarism. They must believe you are my...plaything, so to speak. It won't keep someone from trying to barter for you, but at least they won't steal you. I hope."

He hoped?

"How can they barter for me if you don't want to trade?" I asked.

"They'd go after something I want—something that I might value more. If that doesn't work, they'll just go after something else until they can force me to trade."

"What, you mean like your kid or something?"

"Yes. Or something."

Okay. Now I was officially disgusted by these people.

He continued, "Now, I want you to claw my face and scream loudly."

Whatthehell? "You're serious."

"Yes. Then I will return to the party and you will remain here. With the doors locked until I come to get you."

"And then what?" I asked.

"If all goes well, tonight I will find out who Mack traded the chalice to."

That sounded easy. Too easy.

"Are you ready?" he asked.

"I guess—but first, tell me what happened. How do you feel?"

His eyes filled with conflict and joy. "I feel…whole again."

My eyes filled with a smidgen of tears. I knew I should hate this man for everything he'd done to me, but now I couldn't. He'd been broken before. And now he wasn't.

He took my hand and placed it on his cheek. "Make it bleed."

This was freaking weird. On the other hand, he had gutted me like a fish, cracked my neck a few times, and I think he'd even once lit me on fire. Maybe a few scratches to his beautiful face were in order.

I flexed my fingers and raked down hard, digging my nails into his skin.

He winced and pulled back. "Owww…"

"Seriously?" I sneered at him and then screamed at the top of my lungs.

He gave me a nod and then reminded me not to open the door for anyone except him.

He left, and I locked the doors behind him before plopping down onto the bed. *Well, that was goddamned weird.*

But little did I know, we were just getting started. At the end of it all, each of us would give up a piece of our souls and hearts for the chance to bring Mack back. And one of us would give up everything.

Chapter Twenty

While waiting in the big, expensively decorated bedroom—yes, fit for a king with a king-sized bed, soft down comforter and pillows, and plush velvety white carpet—I realized that I had completely neglected my old life. You know, that one with a job, two retired parents, and a handful of friends who didn't actually know the real me?

Bentley! I dug out my cell from my pocket and called Shannon. Thankfully, Bentley had a doggie door and a big bowl full of food along with water, so he wasn't starving, but who knew when I'd be back.

Come on. Come on. Come on. Yes! Shannon answered, and I told her that I was deathly ill and staying with a friend—which she didn't seem surprised by given how bad off I'd been the last time she'd seen me at the center. I also told her where to find my hidden house key and Bentley's supply of food and treats. I then texted my parents, lying to them too about having the flu, and added a

Facebook post to seal the deal with my friends. I bought myself a few extra days before anyone started really worrying.

After about two hours, I heard a light knock on the door. Unsure of who it might be, I didn't answer.

"It's me, Theodora. They've all left now," said a King-sounding voice.

"How do I know it's really you?"

"You were wearing a brown potato sack and running in the mud the first time I killed you."

Yep. That's King. I went to unlock the door, and he pushed his way in, not pausing to look at me. A man on a mission.

"I found out who Mack traded the chalice to," he said, and began pacing by the window, rubbing that strong stubbled chin of his between his thumb and index finger. Why did he have to look so much like original Mack?

Nature was a cruel teasing bitch to make double.

"And?" I said.

"It's not good. Her name is Talia, and our relationship is less than optimal for a trade of any sort."

"English, please?"

King sighed, and it struck me as odd. He was the sort of man who didn't sigh, whine, whimper or do anything that could possibly be construed as a weakness. He was all about decisive action.

He has really changed. It still shocked the hell out of me that I had the power to do that.

"Talia and I used to be partners," he said. "That

didn't suit her, so I cut ties."

"Oh." I nodded knowingly. "Scorned lover."

"Scorned non-lover. She's vowed to never do a favor for me again until I do one for her." He gave me a look.

"Ah. That kind of favor." These 10 Club women were manipulative, needy sickos.

"Yes. And considering she'll have heard about my escapades with you this evening, she'll be less inclined to change her mind and trade for the chalice."

"Because you slummed it with me, it's a double slap that you wouldn't slum it with her?" I asked sarcastically.

"Precisely," he said, missing the fact that I'd been joking.

"You and I need another dance," I retorted. "Possibly a cha-cha." He needed more of my Seer nice-juice.

He gave me a look. He didn't get it.

"Never mind," I said.

He did just that and continued, "Unfortunately, we will still need to go to Talia and try to strike a deal, as futile as the effort might be. Luckily, I have something she desires."

"More than a chalice?"

"No and yes," he replied.

"Can you be any more vague?" I asked.

"I'm King. I've cornered the market on vague." I heard a phone vibrating somewhere on his body. He slipped his hand into his tux coat pocket and looked at the screen before accepting the call and holding the phone to his ear. "Hello, Miss Turner," he said in a silky, deep voice. He then immediately pulled the device away from his ear. Even I could hear the screaming. After several screechy moments, he turned away from me and cupped the cell to his mouth. "Mia, do not be so foolish. I have not been unfaithful and let me remind you all that I endured to be with you." More screeching and holding the phone from his ear. He then returned it. "Yes. Of course I slept with other women while we were apart. Christ, I was cursed with evil for three thousand years. And I am a man. But this is no reason to accuse me of forsaking my vows." He listened. "Well, if I listened to everything I heard about you, then I might believe you're a whining, annoying, overly curious female. However, I am smarter than most and recognize your inquisitive nature for what it truly is: intelligence and compassion." He listened some more. "Theodora has done nothing more than heal me, Mia. She has taken away my pain and torment." Pause. "Yes. It's true. I merely created an illusion to protect her from the 10 Club." He listened. "Yes, I am wonderful and very strong. You are lucky to have me. Give my love to Arch."

I honestly didn't know what to make of the man. He was still King—all cockiness and powerful—but now he had a less edgier edge.

He ended his call and then put away his cell, looking at me. "So are you ready?"

"Yes—ready for what, though?"

"I am told Talia is in Vegas. We will go to her

and do our best to barter for the chalice."

Vegas. Oh goodie. "If you don't mind my asking, what do you have that she *might* want?"

He looked at me. "She's always wanted a Seer."

"Great."

"But I doubt it will be enough. The chalice is very rare and can bring anyone back from the dead—no matter how old."

"How's that even possible?" I asked, but it was more of a spoken thought. The thing seemed too good to be true.

"They say the great king of the Incas, an expert of the dark arts, used the blood of a thousand priests to mix in with the alloy. He then created a small fissure between our world and the spirit world."

"You just sounded like an episode of the *X-Files*." Yes, I liked the show. Scully was very logical, so it had appealed to the old me.

King shot me a look.

"I'm guessing you're not a TV man," I said.

He lifted his chin proudly. "I watch *Antiques Roadshow*. One must stay current."

I wanted to laugh. Of course he would like that show; he was a three-thousand-year-old antique himself.

"Let us make our way to the airport," he said. "I'll have to procure tickets on the way since I am without a plane or pilot."

I assumed because he'd sent Mia away to Greece with his baby.

"Does Mia have any clothes I could borrow?" I hated to ask, but I was still wearing my black tee, jeans, and tennis shoes from the day before. "And a spare toothbrush?"

"No. She never stays here. She says it gives her the heebie-jeebies. I find the home quite comforting."

Yeah, he'd killed so many nice, nice people on this very spot. Like me! *So homey.*

☞☜

"Please stop threatening to remove people's heads, King. I don't want to end up in jail," I said from inside the fitting room inside the Vegas airport.

His dark voice flowed through the door as if inside the small room with me. I was beginning to learn that while King was no longer a disembodied spirit walking in the world of the living, he still had an abundance of impressive and very spooky powers. Such as being able to project himself into a person's head, mind control, and mass hypnosis. It was a fucking miracle I was still alive because I realized he couldn't kill me just by looking at me.

"I am not that powerful," he said through the other side of the door. "You sound as if you watch too many of the Z-Files."

"*X-Files*. And get out of my head."

"I am merely attempting to ascertain if you plan to double-cross me," he explained.

Why would I do that? I asked.

Because I have decapitated you, disemboweled you, burned you at the stake, and—

Okay. I see your point, I replied. *But get out of*

my head! And he called the passengers on the plane "annoying."

"I will never fly commercial again," he said aloud. "They clearly design those cabins for men without cocks or legs."

I laughed. Sadly, we'd been in a hurry, so he'd purchased seats on Southwest, not understanding this concept of economy-only seating.

"Yes, well, I thought I would simply take a seat in first class. Who invented such a plane without first class? A moron with a vagina, I am guessing."

Still a chauvinist pig. How did Mia put up with him?

"Are you dressed yet?" he asked.

I finished putting on my tennis shoes and opened the door. He looked at me and a tiny smile flickered across his lips.

I looked down at my slot-machine sweater, complete with a sequin handle. "It's all they have, King."

He chuckled and followed me to the register so I could pay. I had to admit, seeing this different version of King—less callous, less serious—really made my heart ache that much more for Mack. I imagined how he might be if he weren't carrying around all that baggage and self-loathing.

About forty minutes later, we were sitting in a suite called a Skyloft at the MGM. I'd never seen a hotel room that looked more like a five-star, modern townhouse slash nightclub with a view of Vegas.

"This Talia must be a high roller," I said, looking out the two-story-high windows on the top floor of the high-rise hotel.

"When one has powers such as hers, gambling is just an easy way to make money."

I understood that he meant she had her ways of winning, just like King had his ways of finding people and then convincing the bellhop to let us in to wait for our "friend."

"Well, well, well," said a sugary-sweet voice from the black lacquered double doors. "What brings the infamous King to my kingdom of sin?"

I looked at the woman and honestly didn't know what to think. She had shiny long brown hair, was about my height—five seven—and weighed about a hundred pounds from the look of her. But her anorexic frame wasn't what had me gawking. Lord, that face. Her skin was so tight from too many face-lifts, I was sure her cheekbones were going to pop out underneath the inch of pancake makeup she wore.

"Cut the bullshit, Talia," he said in a cold, menacing tone, showing no signs of his recent change of heart. "You know why I'm here."

"I can guess." She dipped her head. "You're looking for your brother."

So Talia didn't know Mack was dead. I assumed King wasn't going to share either.

"No," King said. "I am looking for something he stole from me. Something he then traded with you."

She cackled into the air, then withdrew a cigarette from her shiny gold handbag and lit it up. "Well, then you're wasting your time, King. Because I traded with him fair and square, per the rules of the 10 Club." She blew out a big puff of smoke.

King stepped in. "It's mine, Talia. I need it for another trade."

She laughed and shook her head. "Don't treat me like an idiot. I know you want the thing for your sweet little Mia." She rolled her eyes. "God, I should've choked her when I had the chance."

King didn't react to the jab. I held my breath, waiting to see where this would go.

King shook his head condescendingly. "Since we both know you don't need the chalice because you have no one you care for or who's ever cared for you—alive or dead—why don't you name your price so I can be on my way, Talia."

A sinister rage flickered in her eyes. "I want Miranda taken out and myself appointed as the new president of 10 Club."

His blue, blue eyes flickered. "You know that I am merely a member. I cannot grant such a thing."

From the way she cocked a badly drawn eyebrow, I could see she didn't believe him. "You and I both know you can make things happen—you have influence among the other members."

King shook his head. "You wouldn't last a day as president—the other members will kill you before the announcement goes out."

She glared at him. "I wasn't done yet." Meaning, she had more demands?

"Go on." King crossed his thick arms.

"I want you."

He scoffed. "Never going to happen."

"Why? Because you married that little Seer cunt."

I could tell that comment got under his skin. Deep, deep under. Jaw flexing, fists clenching hard.

"No," he replied. "Because you are a vile, treacherous woman and my dick would rather shrivel up and fall off than enter that three-hundred-year-old rotting hole you call a vagina."

Ouch! That had to hurt. Good one, King. I hoped he was listening in on my thoughts. *Wait—she's three hundred years old?*

She cocked her head to the side, almost as if she knew she had him by the balls. "That's my price, King. Take it or leave it."

He stared at her, unflinching.

Oh, God. He's not actually considering her offer, is he? I needed to intervene.

"I think it would be pretty humiliating to have a man's dick literally fall off at the sight of you." Talia shot poison darts from her eyes at me. "What? Just sayin'." I shrugged. "Also saying that Seers are extremely rare. Would you want one as a trade instead?"

"Theodora," King barked, "you are to remain silent."

But...wasn't that the plan? Trading me? I thought.

Silence, he projected into my head.

Talia lifted a brow and then took a good hard look at me. "A Seer," she said with delight. "I thought you killed them all, King. Except for your Mia of course, who I hear is no longer useful. Just had to break her, didn't you?"

Given my and King's history, I wasn't shocked by hearing he had killed Seers. I just wondered why. *A question for another day.*

"Well," he said, "I clearly have not killed them all, but I am not willing to part with this one." He gave me a shushing glance, urging me to keep my mouth shut.

Talia shrugged. "Suit yourself. My terms still stand if you want the chalice."

What the hell had just happened? Because if I didn't know any better, I'd say that King had…protected me again, like he had at the party. Yes. This man who'd hunted me and hated me for killing his brother was now saving me from whatever horrible fate might become of me if I were to be given to this woman.

"Show me the chalice," King said.

"Wait." I grabbed his elbow. "Can we talk? Outside?"

The nostrils on King's perfectly straight, regal nose flared with contempt.

"It's important," I urged.

He narrowed his beautiful eyes at me, which reminded me of why he was doing this: Mack. And while Mia had not gone into detail, the fact that she was willing to save Mack versus her own brother, simply based on the fact that King could not live without his twin, spoke volumes. She knew that these two brothers were clearly joined at the hip and had been for eons. Honestly, I was an only child, but I could still relate. I felt the same way about

Mack as King did.

"It better be important, Miss Valentine, or I will be forced to punish you," King said.

I wanted to kick his shins for that comment, but my Seer goggles told me this was all an act. The colors bursting from his body were vivid greens and white. Not that I'd figured out what any of it meant, but looking at him literally made me feel good.

I lifted my chin, playing along. "That's Dr. Valentine, King."

He dipped his head. "Very well, *Dr. Valentine*, you have two minutes."

I followed him out the door into the hall. Once the door was closed, I went into hysterics. "What are you doing, King?" I hissed.

"Saving my brother," he hissed back.

"Then do it," I barked. "Trade me like you said you would. I don't care." Mack was everything to me.

"He will never forgive me if he returns and finds you are the property of Talia. This is the only way."

"No." I fumed. "You will just have to tell Mack that I did this for him, because he would never forgive me for ruining his brother's life."

"I am over three thousand fucking years old, Miss Valentine. I will not let some second-rate, pre-Colombian voodoo queen Seer tell me what to do."

What! "Yes, you will."

He lowered his head, just inches from my face and then waved his hand across it. "Yes...*You*...Will..."

His words seeped into my skull like the memory

of delicious fresh baked cookies—so welcome and irresistible. Suddenly, I wanted to do everything he said.

He added, "And you will wait out here for me in silence until I retrieve you."

The front part of my lobe made me nod and say, "Yes. I will wait here." The back part of my lobe was kicking and cursing—*A-hole! A-hole! A-hole!*—totally helpless to override his command.

He walked away, leaving me just standing there in the hallway like a useless clump of mashed potatoes. *He can't do this, he can't*, I thought.

But he did. And there was absolutely nothing I could do about it.

Chapter Twenty-One

I didn't know how much time passed, but when King grabbed my hand and began tugging me toward the elevators, I immediately saw the blue light seeping from his body into the air around him.

That can't be good.

"You okay?" I asked as we rode down in the elevator.

"Why wouldn't I be?" He lifted his chin a little.

"Because if you just did what I think you did, your dick is in the process of shriveling up." I'd meant that as a joke, but given my lack of experience in that department, I immediately regretted my choice. Clearly, the man was upset.

Then it dawned on me: my gift. I reached out and placed my hand on his, attempting to duplicate the healing process from earlier. Nothing happened.

"It's not working," I said, pulling away and inspecting my hands.

"Some pain cannot be erased," he said regretfully. "Nor should they be."

Meaning, he wanted to suffer? Meaning he actually did *it*? "Oh, God. Please don't tell me…No. No. Not with her."

He looked straight ahead at the doors. "I did what I had to."

"You didn't…" His wife would be devastated. I mean, if Mack screwed Talia after marrying me and my having his child, there would be no excuse on earth that could wash away my pain or prevent me from removing his dangly parts with my fingernails. That wasn't to say that I wouldn't understand the why. But could I live with it or forgive it? No. Not when I loved him so deeply and passionately. There could be no sharing for any reason when you've given your heart so completely to another.

"Thank you, Theodora," King said sarcastically, replying to my thoughts.

"Sorry. But there's right and then there's real. Real is never wanting to share the person you're in love with. I mean, could you forgive Mia if she slept with Mack to save your life?"

He swiveled his head in my direction and snarled.

"Exactly," I said. "But…" I shook my head. "Did you really…do…that?" I still couldn't believe it.

"I do not wish to discuss this."

The doors slid open, and we stepped out of the elevator to make our way to the awaiting limo outside. After we got in, King murmured, "You will have to make Mia understand, Theodora. Make her understand how much I love her. She will listen to you. Seers have a special bond." The heart-wrenching sorrow in his tone was almost too much to bear.

Crap. I think I'm going to cry.

I scrubbed my face with my hands. "I'm not a magician. I can't just make her feel happy—or—I don't know." I sighed. "Maybe I can." This was all still so new to me. "But...Okay, don't get pissy on me for saying this, King, but you're King. People fear you. You squash anything that gets in your way. Why didn't you fight?"

"Who says I didn't?" He cleared his throat and straightened his tie.

"Meaning?"

"Talia has upped her game. I was unprepared." King's aura instantly turned to a dark blue. This mood-ring feature was very strange.

I frowned at him, wondering what the ever-living hell that meant. Then it dawned on me; the little tidbits I'd heard and seen. These 10 Club people were ruthless.

I gasped and covered my mouth. "She has something on you, doesn't she?"

"Not on. Over," he corrected solemnly.

I heard the wheels in my head go *click!-click!-click!* Talia had leverage on him. And the only thing King loved more than Mack was likely his wife and baby son.

Reading my thoughts, King said, "And you would be correct in your assumption."

Fucking bitch. I didn't know the details, but what did that matter? Talia had backed King into a corner so dark and tight that he'd had no choice.

King's head whipped in my direction. "Don't. You. Say. A fucking word, Seer. Or so help me I will disembowel you. Are we clear?"

I nodded stiffly. "I'll do my best to make Mia understand." I slid my hand over his and gave it a squeeze. I think that was the moment that I realized that hate and revenge were like unwelcome viruses in my soul. I was built to forgive and heal. And now, more than ever, I wanted to make King's pain dissolve but couldn't. And it was a strange, strange thing wanting to help this man. He'd been my nemesis for an eternity. Now I felt protective of him like a big sister. "I'll do everything I can to make things right. I promise."

⁓⋄⁓

Six hours later, around nine in the morning, King and I were back at his San Francisco palace, making preparations to resurrect Mack. And once again, I had to keep my head from exploding. It had been a week—yes, only one week—since I'd first laid eyes on Mack. My entire life changed in that moment. *I* changed in that moment. And I guessed that was only the tip of the iceberg. Because, yes, I had regained the part of myself that felt connected to this world, but I still couldn't remember my past. I suspected that once I fixed that, it would open up yet another whole new world for me—how to control my gift, the feelings that I had for those I loved in my past lives, the lessons I'd learned along the way.

But for now, I had to take stock of the vast metamorphosis I'd undergone in just seven little days. No light, no love, no passion in my life to now...*Performing resurrection rituals to bring back the love of my existence.* I almost laughed. Almost. *Nope, not one bit of logic or the old Teddi in this room.*

According to an ancient text King'd procured "many dark lifetimes ago" he'd said, there were specific steps that had to be followed to open the fissure between worlds and beckon a soul to return. Once the soul arrived, somehow a body...appeared. Or something. That was where his plan became a bit—okay, really, really vague.

"Sooo..." I said, pacing back and forth in King's living room, the same living room that had been filled with 10 Club members yesterday evening and had been cleaned spotless. Probably by one of King's people possessions. "You are going to bring Mack back and put him into his old body?"

"Maybe," he said, completely absorbed in is preparation of the five-foot-wide, witchy-looking circle he'd drawn with blood in the center of his hardwood floor—an outrageous cliché. He'd finally removed his bow tie and had rolled up his sleeves to avoid getting messy, but there were smatters of blood and some ashy stuff smudged on his face and shirt.

"I'm going to take that to mean you're not sure," I said.

Kneeling, he adjusted the small silver chalice so that these little arrow-like symbols on the sides lined up with markers on the circle. "Maybe."

I lifted both brows. "Really? You're going to wing it?"

His head of dark shiny hair whipped up, and his cobalt eyes burrowed into me. "Have a better idea, Dr. Valentine?"

I mashed my lips together. "Nope."

"Then please be quiet. I'm trying to concentrate."

"Fine. Okay." I blew out a long breath, hoping this would work. After all that we'd been through, this would be the end of a very, very long journey for Mack, myself, and for King. No more curses. No more killing. Just living and being happy. I only hoped I could help Mia overcome King's very disturbing infidelity. Basically, he'd been…ugh…forced to choose between not only Mack, but Mia and his child too.

Dear God, what does Talia have hanging over this man?

Whatever it was, getting Mia's heart to heal wouldn't be easy. *She'll be hurt regardless.*

"Not helping, Theodora." King twisted the small silver cup a little to the right.

"Sorry." *But you really should stay out of my head.*

"Not likely—I've been doing it for so long, it's almost involuntary." He got to his feet and stared down at his handiwork. "The wait is over. If I've done this correctly, Mack will appear as soon as we place an article of his inside the chalice." King took a silver necklace with an Egyptian ankh from his pocket and placed it inside the cup. That had to be the necklace Mack told me about. I guessed King had tracked it down—probably not too difficult for a man like him if he truly was as good at finding things as Mia had said.

"I am better than good," King said, correcting my thoughts. "And now for the blood of an innocent baby."

I gasped. "What?"

"Relax." He frowned. "I called in a favor and procured some from a stillborn."

My mouth turned down at its corners. "What is *wrong* with you people?"

"Do you prefer we take the blood from a living, healthy infant?"

Wincing, I said, "No. But..."

"But nothing. The infant's life will serve a greater purpose, and no harm came to him on our account."

Trying not to be sick, I flicked my wrists through the air. "Just...hurry—get it over with." Not like he needed my permission, but I wasn't going anywhere and I was beyond anxious.

He walked over to the bar in the corner and ducked behind it, reemerging with a small bag of blood. He then returned to the circle and knelt beside it, his finely featured face turning into an oasis of serenity. Eyes closed, he began chanting in an ancient language that reminded me of Hebrew with lots of deep-throated phlegm-like sounds. He then opened his eyes and squeezed the syrupy contents into the silver chalice. Surprisingly, the chalice wasn't this huge goblet-like thing I'd imagined it to be. In fact, it reminded me of those small glasses used for sherry only this one was made of metal.

The room immediately began to glow and then the walls around us started pulsing and throbbing as if we were inside some sort of heart.

But as I watched the chalice, I noticed its form dissolving. "What's happening?"

King stopped his voodoo chatter and stared down at the thing with outrage. "Fucking Mack!"

"What? What!"

"It's a fake," he groaned.

No. No. Noooo... I covered my face. *Mack, what in the world did you do with it?*

※

King and I sat in his sleek, stainless-steel-everything chef's kitchen, sulking at the black granite breakfast bar, sipping copious amounts of scotch. Yes, for breakfast. After all, it was eleven in the morning and we needed some sort of fuel for our long day of misery ahead.

"You gonna answer that?" I slurred.

King's cell phone kept ringing. It had to be Mia. *Poor guy*. I couldn't blame him for not wanting to have *that* conversation, but eventually, he would have to face her along with the fact that he'd been forced to fuck a woman he loathed for a forged chalice. It was a sad, sad moment for this man, and I couldn't help but feel sorry for him.

"Please don't remind me," he grumbled in reply to my thoughts.

Sorry. "So do you think Talia switched the chalice?" I asked.

"No. She would not knowingly give me a fake." Still in his dirty tux, he poured another tall glass of scotch into his glass tumbler, his head sagging a bit.

I sipped on my second glass and bobbed my head. "Well, Miranda said that Mack gave her a phony chalice, too." She'd chucked it at his head. "That means Mack made two fakes and the real one is out there."

"Aren't you the sharp one," he grumbled.

Oh, shut up. I took a swig of scotch.

"Of course," King continued, thinking aloud, half mumbling, "something so rare and powerful would have to be kept in a safe place."

"Maybe he didn't trade it at all," I said, the thought slamming into my skull like a falling brick. It was simply a hunch. But considering Mack's story about the first time we met, I knew how determined he'd been to make his way back to Minoa with that rock. He loved his brother, and Mia I assumed, and would've wanted them to have the real chalice after he'd gotten what he wanted and double-crossed a few very powerful and scary people. The question was, where had Mack hidden it?

That is, if I'm right.

I looked at King. "Now that I'm thinking about it, he kept saying something about being warm or buried somewhere warm. Does that mean anything?"

King's beautiful face contorted into a very unpleasant-looking and nasty snarl. "I am going to kill you, Theodora. But this time it will be for pure and simple pleasure."

I instinctively leaned away in my chair. Not that it would do any good. At best, I'd make it to the other side of the kitchen if King wanted me dead. Anyway, I took his reaction to mean that Mack had given me some sort of code. Still…

"Screw you, King. The man I love was bleeding out in my arms, gasping for air. It kind of overshadowed the freaking moment. So where is the chalice, then?"

"My brother was likely trying to say that he was 'keeping it warm'—a phrase we used as children when we took something from each other without asking. I would catch him red-handed, playing with my hunting blade, and he would simply say he was merely 'keeping it warm for me.' I would take his bows, and when he caught me, I'd say the same thing."

I swallowed hard, fully understanding what this meant. Mack had had it on him somewhere, which given the leather jacket he'd worn was entirely possible. The cup wasn't all that big and he could've easily had it tucked inside a pocket. I never would've noticed since I'd only seen him wear the jacket when he'd been in my backseat. After that, he'd taken it off, but I had no clue where that jacket went.

"Did you happen to see his leather jacket at the cabin?" I asked.

King rubbed his forehead and groaned. "I laid it over him when we buried him. That was his favorite jacket."

"And you buried him…?"

"In that ancient burial ground. It was the only place that had ever given him peace without having to kill."

Crap. It was one thing to have to watch Mack die, but it would be an entirely different breed of horror returning to the scene of the crime and watching King dig him up.

Seriously. I need to track down whoever erased my memories. I was beginning to wonder if they'd only been doing me a favor.

༺༻

Unwilling to once again brave the "deplorable conditions" of commercial airlines—King's words—or risk his necessary "supplies" for the ritual being touched by anyone, we made the nine-hour drive back to that cabin in the desert. For the first hour of the trip, I had to listen to King curse the gods of ancient Greece because his helicopter was somewhere on the East Coast. Then the next four hours, the car—a black Mercedes sedan with tinted windows—was filled with a dreadful silence, interrupted by his phone ringing every five minutes.

"If you're not going to answer it, why don't you shut it off?" I finally asked around five in the afternoon, on my last leg of any civilized emotions.

His blue eyes, with eagle-like intensity, remained focused on the road. "I am waiting for a very important call."

"I see." I glanced his way and noticed how he had a blue light all around him.

"What do all of the colors mean?" I asked.

He looked at me for a brief moment and then brought his eyes back to the road. "Every Seer is different, I'm told, but red is anger, hate, rage, and pain. Black is death. Green is life."

"What about blue?"

"Sorrow and regret."

"That's what I thought."

His phone rang again and the name "Mia" popped up on the screen of the center console.

"Avoiding her is only making it worse," I said. "She's probably worried."

"I am aware of this," he replied coldly.

"Just answer it. Tell her what happened. I'm sure that the not knowing is torturing her."

King sneered. "This, coming from you, is rich."

"Why?"

"Haven't you wondered why you cannot remember your past?" he asked.

"Of course."

"Because you couldn't take it anymore—this truth you speak so fondly of. It was too much for you."

He had to be messing with me, but that look on his face said otherwise. "So what did I do?"

"Fifty years ago, I tracked you down in London.

Your Seer gift was just beginning to awaken, as were your memories. This is how I always knew you were coming—your thoughts become quite loud. And because you're connected to Mack, and I to him, it's not hard for someone of my particular skill set and background to find you."

I bobbed my head and looked out the window at the winter sun dipping below the horizon without fanfare or glitz. Quiet. Melancholy. Just like me. I didn't like where this story was going.

He continued, "But this time, before I took your head, you didn't fight, you didn't cry. You simply begged me to give you a moment. You said you couldn't bear it anymore."

"Bear what?" I asked with a dreaded sigh.

"I wasn't sure what you did at the time—but now I know that your gift is healing. You healed yourself the only way you could: by making yourself forget everything. Mack, me, your past."

I was completely stunned—yet, I kind of wasn't. Probably because somewhere in the back of my mind, I already knew what he'd just told me.

"But I didn't forget—not really," I said.

He shrugged. "It is like I told you; some emotions are meant to be felt. We cannot truly erase them."

I finally understood. I'd tried to block it all out, but it hadn't worked. I was a Seer. Ancient. Powerful. Connected to everything. And asking myself to forget Mack was like asking myself to forget my own soul or who I was. At the end of the day, I could never change or destroy what was inside my heart. It was part of me. So seeing Mack, gazing into his eyes, had restored the piece of me connected to him. It could never be erased. It had only been buried below the surface, just waiting for the right catalyst. My memories—those moments in time that were stored in my brain—well, those were gone.

I laughed out loud, chuckling toward the ceiling of the car and smacking my knee. "It's ironic, isn't it? I tried to heal myself, but ended up being more broken than ever."

"You simply wanted to be free of your own pain," King said. "I can relate. Regardless, after that, you couldn't remember a thing. I ended up sparing your life and using your gifts for a while."

My jaw dropped. "Well, that was kind of rude."

He shrugged. "Waste not, want not. I ended up killing you anyway."

"Gee. Thanks."

"You may have forgotten your past, but you were still just as stubborn and disobedient as always. You ended up crossing paths with Mack one day—you were supposed to be out at a job, but decided to show up at my townhouse in London. I quickly got rid of you."

"Didn't it bother you? Killing me over and over again?" I asked.

"No. I was fighting my own demons. And, as you're aware, there's nothing I won't do for my brother. He is my blood. We've also established that lost memories or not, you are a hazard to him, which is why I still intend to kill you after we've brought him back and you've healed him."

I hissed out a breath. "You're a ruthless asshole, you know that?"

He dipped his head. "So I've been told."

"If we bring Mack back, he'll be free from my father's curse. And I never vowed to kill him, only to free him. My curse or promise or whatever you call it will be ended, too."

"Are you certain?" he asked.

I gave it some thought. "It has to be over at that point, King."

"I am not willing to risk it."

Seriously? "Well, I sure as hell am not going to let you murder me again, King—and has it ever crossed your mind that this is all your fault? That in your quest to protect Mack, you're actually being extremely selfish? You can't stand the thought of losing him, so you destroyed him. You keep killing the woman he loves—and by the way, you no longer have the excuse of being an evil disembodied bastard. I mean, for fuck's sake, King, how would you feel if Mack kept killing Mia in the name of brotherly love? But somehow, Mack still loved you. And he forgave you. Again and again. Probably out of guilt because of what he did to you three-thousand-fucking-who-cares years ago. But you! You just keep hurting him with your high-handed 'I know what's best for my brother' bullcrap, which is probably why he wanted to die. He couldn't take watching me bite the dust anymore and he couldn't turn his back on you." I threw up my hands. "Just let the fucking man live in peace, King! Let me and him figure out how to fix this."

King glanced at me with those cold blue eyes, but didn't say a word.

"Fine," I said. "But then don't ask me to help you win back Mia. She can divorce your evil ass for all I care."

King snapped his mouth shut and growled.

"Oh. Did you forget about that?" I asked. "Your wife who's going to be heartbroken? You'll be lucky if you ever get near her or your son again."

A long, frigid moment passed.

"Perhaps," King cleared his throat, "we can come to an agreement of sorts."

I huffed and crossed my arms over my chest. "Yep. That's what I thought."

Point for Teddi.

Chapter Twenty-Two

When we pulled down that long dirt road shrouded in an eerie, foreboding energy meant to keep curious eyes away, I now had the distinct impression that King's little tricks weren't the only thing safeguarding these grounds.

"There are many souls watching over this land," King said, reading my thoughts.

His Mercedes rumbled down the road, the wheels crunching and grinding the dirt.

"Stay out of my head!" I barked over the loud noise. "And how the hell did you and Mack find this place to begin with?"

"The place has power and is considered to be one of my possessions. I protect this land, and in exchange, the souls who reside here assist me from time to time."

"Like some kind of ghost brotherhood?"

King smiled in a sinister sort of way. "Something like that."

"So why did Mack want to be buried here?"

King's smile faded.

"Tell me," I prodded.

We pulled up to the rickety shack, and King turned off the engine. "Because he wanted to be with you. We buried your bodies here—a few anyway."

I blinked at him. *Jeez. How morbid. And why did you even care where my body went?*

King stared ahead, his eyes locked on the cabin, though he clearly wasn't looking at it.

I waited. "Why, King?"

"Because this place is where souls who die with honor are laid to rest."

I stared at the side of his face, unable to truly believe what this man had just said. "But you hunted me. You ruthlessly murdered me."

He cleared his throat. "I did what I had to do to keep my brother alive. And I would do it again. But that doesn't mean I discounted the love he had for you."

I looked away and my eyes followed a little dust devil spinning next to my door. This was possibly the strangest confession I'd ever heard. King had ended my life and then taken great care to bury me somewhere he clearly felt was special.

"Errr. Thanks. That was very thoughtful of you. In a very cold-blooded kind of way."

"Don't mention it." King nodded but didn't look at me. Regardless, the torment in his eyes was obvious. "Let us get to work." He opened the car door.

"Wait!"

King had already gotten out, so he bent over and looked at me through the open driver door.

"I can't," I said. "I can't watch you dig him up." The thought of looking at his pale, lifeless face was too much.

"I understand. I will return shortly." He closed the door, and I watched that tall frame—now dressed in black jeans and a thin black sweater—disappear behind the cabin. From where I sat, yes, still wearing my stupid Vegas sweater, I saw nothing but a plain dirt field with rolling hills off in the distance. My guess was that there was a cemetery back there that could only be seen by certain people. Kind of like the inside of that cabin.

This place is so freaking weird.

Over a half an hour passed until King returned, the sleeves of his black sweater pushed up and his jeans covered in dirt. The icy look on his exotically sculpted face, a face I still saw as Mack's, was undecipherable.

I popped open my door and hopped out. "Did he have it?" I asked anxiously.

King nodded his head of thick black hair.

"Yes!" I slammed the car door and did a little celebratory air box. We were going to get Mack back. *But what's with Mr. Dark and Dreary over there?*

"Please, don't tell me you have bad news," I said.

King shook his head, and that was when I noticed deep blues shedding off him as if he were melting.

"Whatthefuck?" I whispered under my breath.

King ignored me. "Come. I have him wrapped in cloth. We can perform the ceremony outside behind the cabin. Please grab the cooler from the trunk. It's underneath Mack's duffel bag."

Cooler. There's a cooler of...Don't think about it! "You need to consider changing your profession, King. This is just not right."

He dipped his head. "Rome wasn't built in a day, Miss Valentine." He disappeared behind the cabin once again, and I went to pop the trunk. Of course, I had to snoop in the bag.

I unzipped the thing and found clean clothes. It was a touchingly sweet thing to do, bringing fresh clothes for his brother. It was a sign of how much he cared.

I shoved the clothes back inside and zipped up the bag, going for the…the…cooler of…

Supplies. They are just supplies. What sort of people were these Incas that they'd make this blood part of the—

Any day now, Miss Valentine, I heard King's voice resonate inside my brain.

I blew out a breath, prepared for anything. Okay, that was a lie. I wasn't prepared for this at all.

༺༻

Like before, King created a circle of blood with little symbols around it. Only now I realized that it wasn't some satanic circle of resurrection, but a compass or a sundial meant to properly orient the chalice.

"So it's like a combination lock," I said aloud, completely fascinated.

"Precisely," King said, once again down on his knees, fine-tuning the strange etching on the side of the chalice, which wasn't really what I would call a holy grail or anything of the sort. It looked like a miniature wineglass made of metal.

Mack's body was only a few feet away, wrapped in a white sheet. I could barely breathe anytime I looked at it. Truthfully, I could understand why I would heal myself and wipe away my memories. Some things were simply too painful to live with for an eternity, and watching Mack die was one of them. I guessed that was part of the reason he didn't want to stick around either. He'd had to watch me go more than once and several of those times by his brother's hand. Yet, he always remained loyal to King, despite all of the horrific things he'd done while cursed. Maybe because Mack was in no position to throw stones. And his heart was just really, really big.

King rose, dusting off his hands. "All right. It's ready."

I handed him the cooler, and he repeated the same bizarre ritual as before with the blood, the necklace, and the chanting. But this time, something different happened. The sky above us turned a deep purple and the wind kicked up, filling the air around us with several hissing dust devils.

"What's happening?" I said loudly over the noise.

"The spirits are unhappy. They don't want to let Mack through."

I guessed if anyone would know that, it would be an ex-ghost. "What do we do?"

King mashed his lips together, and then his eyes locked on me. "Come here. Give me your hands."

I didn't want to because I knew I couldn't trust this man, despite his now being healed. He was still ruled by a moral compass entirely his own, and loyalty to his blood was top priority.

"I give you my word; I won't harm you. Yet."

Damn that man. Always reading my thoughts.

"Fine." I stepped around the circle and held out my hands.

"Very good," King said. "Now, I want you to focus on your gift and try to move that light through me."

"It didn't work the last time!" I yelled over the growing hisses and whipping wind.

"The healing is not for me," he explained. "I believe they're upset. They don't understand why it can't be their turn."

They were freaking jealous. Dear God, how crazy was all this?

King grabbed my wrists and closed his eyes, telling me to focus on healing them and helping them to rest. So I imagined that ball of white light somewhere beyond my body, existing in a place beyond this one, and then began pulling from it. Slowly, I felt the draw. The light moving through me like a warm, comforting stream of bathwater.

I realized that like that chalice, my body was merely a conduit, a door with a combination lock that when opened could connect two energies together. When the light hit my fingers and flowed into King, I actually felt it continuing on through him and out another door. It was the spirit world that King lived in for thousands of years.

And then...I felt them.

Ohmygod! My eyes snapped open and met King's.

"You were doing well, do not stop," he commanded.

"Mack never crossed over. He never left," I said in a panic. "They wouldn't let him."

"What?" King looked pissed. And surprised.

"And they don't want to be healed," I added. "They just want a sacrifice."

King frowned. Now he looked really pissed.

"Nothing comes without a price," I elaborated. "It's that cosmic balance thing! Shit—I don't know what you call it." And I don't know how I knew all that, but I did.

King dropped his hands and looked down at the ground. Meanwhile, my mind had a go at the puzzle pieces. They wanted a sacrifice. Meaning...someone had to take his—

Oh fuck. I stepped back, but King caught my arm, and I suddenly couldn't move. Nor could I speak or breathe or do anything other than realize I would become the sacrificial lamb.

Please, King. There has to be another way, I

pleaded in my head. *If you kill me, you'll have brought your brother back just to let him suffer. He won't forgive himself unless I heal him.*

King continued staring at me with those piercing orbs of endless blue.

Blue. So much blue. And then darker and darker.

"You're right; there is another way, Miss Valentine." He dropped his firm grip and slid off a silver ring from his right index finger. The ring was chunky with a clear stone in the middle. I'd never even noticed him wearing it.

"Take this and put it on," he said.

It was far too large for my hand, but who the hell cared? "What are you doing?" I frowned.

"It will make me feel better knowing that you'll always be around to watch over my brother." He grabbed my left hand and shoved the thing into my palm, practically crushing my poor little fingers as he forced me to make a fist around it.

"What the—" I was about to jerk my hand away, but as King held my hand in his, I could see him. Really see him. All the way down to his soul. And it was literally breaking apart, as if dissolving.

I covered my mouth with my free hand. Unable to bear the sight of what I was witnessing: a man breaking. Truly and utterly breaking, realizing he would never find real peace or happiness or be able to save the people he needed most in this world. But that was what my Seer gift showed me. King's heart ripping apart, disintegrating into dark ash. And as I realized what he meant to do, my heart broke right along with his.

Mack

You can't do that, King. Please don't. Think of Mia and your baby. Think of how lost Mack will be without you. We'll find another way, I promise. The tears fell from my eyes in steady streams, dribbling down my cheeks.

"It's been a pleasure, Dr. Valentine." King dipped his head of silky black hair, and then I watched the dark shadows, in the shape of arms, spring from the ground and reach for his legs. He collapsed to the ground.

"No!" I jumped on top of him and rolled him flat on his back, frantically checking for a pulse.

Nothing.

"Fuckingshit, King! Don't do this!" I puffed several breaths into his mouth and then began pumping his chest. "You evil stubborn bastard! Mack won't want this!"

Minutes or hours went by—I didn't know—but the dust devils died down, and the sky turned to a pristine blue. There was a sudden warmth in the air and sweet smell in the wind blowing through my hair. It was the scent of peace. That was all I knew.

And then I felt lighter. Not physically, but…well, mentally. Like there had been a weight—guilt, despair, fear—pressing down on me that was suddenly gone.

My own curse—that vow I'd made so many years ago—was gone.

"It's useless, you know," said a deep familiar voice. "That fucking prick just had to be the hero."

I gasped and turned my head, finding a tall, naked man, ripped from head to toe with glossy black, shoulder-length hair. He looked just like King with those stunning sky-colored eyes, thick dark lashes, sensual mouth, black stubble and…

A sadness in his eyes.

"Mack?" My voice came out all shaky.

"Yes."

"Ohmygod." I jumped up and ran to him, throwing my arms around his neck. I kissed him with everything I had—my heart, my soul, and every ounce of passion. He kissed me back, and yes, he was buck naked, but this wasn't that kind of moment or that kind of kiss. It was pure and simple, a need to be touched and held and comforted. It was two people testing their sanity to ensure that what was in front of them was real.

After several long moments, I pulled away, my eyes tearing like crazy. "Is it gone? The curse?"

He nodded. "Yes. Though, I'm not exactly sure how, because I couldn't move past this place. I felt it clinging to me until the very last moment." He looked behind me at his dead brother lying in the dirt. "I think…"

Saying that he looked sad would be the understatement of the century. He looked absolutely devastated.

"I'm so sorry, Mack. I tried to stop him."

"I know. I saw the whole thing," he said.

"You did?" I sniffled.

He nodded. "Yes, and I should've known my brother wouldn't let me go peacefully."

"But we can use the chal…" My words faded along with the idea as I noticed that the chalice was gone, a small crater left in its place. *Ohgod. Where did it go?* I blew out a breath, trying to hold it together. I was crushed for Mack, yet I was elated to have him back. Did that make me greedy or uncaring? I didn't know. But all I could do was look at this beautiful man who'd I'd loved before this version of me was even born. It was all too surreal for words.

I stared in wonder at this new perfect body that looked just like his original.

"You can't stare at me like that. Not here," Mack said.

I cleared my throat. "Let's get you some clothes."

Never in a million years would I begin to understand how something like that chalice worked, so I would end up doing myself a favor and simply calling it magic. Later, much, much later, Mack would try to explain it in terms of particle theory, matter cohesion, and energy fields, which normally would've rung my brainy-bell, but was still too outlandish and landed me back in the "magic bucket." For the time being, however, none of that would matter, because the facts were the facts: We buried King that day, right alongside Mack's old body. Mack was heartbroken, but wasn't ready to let me heal him from this or any of his painful baggage from the past. Watching him bury his twin was the saddest moment I could remember living through.

"What are you going to tell Mia?" I asked, wishing that I could be there in Greece when she heard the news that the man who'd loved her for three thousand years was dead. Again.

Mack looked deeply troubled as he scratched the back of his head. "I'm going to tell her the truth. All of it."

I grabbed his hand and gave it a gentle squeeze. "Is there anything I can do?"

"Drive me to the airport and then wait for me."

I looked at him, trying to puzzle it out.

"I must tell her the news face to face," he elaborated.

"I should go with you."

"No. I want to do this alone. But I will let her know you are there to help if she needs it."

I had to wonder if part of the reason he didn't want me there was that Mia might feel I was responsible in some way. Had I not killed Mack, none of this would've happened. I hoped that wasn't the case, but if it gave her any sort of comfort, I could live with taking the blame.

We got into the car and drove away with Mack at the wheel. And I swear, as crazy as it sounded, I felt like someone was watching us until we hit the main road.

"Mack? Do you think King will find a way back again?"

He shook his head. "This isn't like before when he had hope of seeing Mia again and lifting his curse. She won't ever be able to look at him again when she finds out about Talia, no matter the reason."

Yes, I had told Mack everything that happened,

everything we went through to get that chalice. He wasn't happy about it, but the fact that King was willing to sacrifice everything—his marriage, his family, his dream of happiness, and his life—was a testament to how deeply he cared and how deeply he loved.

It left me speechless, frankly. And it made me realize how big these two men's hearts truly were.

I looked away from Mack and focused my teary eyes on the road. "There has to be a way to get him back," I muttered, half-thinking aloud.

"The spirits who sit on that land will never let him leave. A deal was struck, and it's irrevocable. He has the choice to pass over to the other side or stay there."

If anyone would know, it was Mack.

"Still," he said, "I won't ever stop trying."

With a bond like these two brothers had, it was something I didn't doubt.

Chapter Twenty-Three

Two weeks later.

I didn't hear much from Mack after he left for Crete, except for a few text messages here and there to let me know he was with Mia, doing his best to help her come to terms with everything. I could see that he felt responsible for her Archon in his brother's absence. Once again, I volunteered to get on a plane to ease her pain, but I think Mack and I both knew, just like King had, that some pain was meant to be felt. Sometimes it was simply a byproduct of that definitive moment when our hearts had to let go of something that could never be returned. Infidelity, death, betrayal—when these things came into our lives, we hurt because we lost someone or something we loved, leaving behind a hole. But it was also the moment our healing started. You had to feel pain in order to move forward.

But now, back at home in Santa Barbara, trying

to sort out the pieces of my life—or existence, really—I needed Mack. Without him, I found it difficult to look forward. The past kept calling me, reaching its dark tentacles over thousands of years, my mind trying to cope with the blank spaces where memories once belonged. Still, I did my best to focus on how lucky I was to have Mack back. It wasn't perfect, but life rarely is, and I could think of no better joy than "making do" with this man.

As for work, everyone assumed that Mr. Room Twenty-Five had run off on his own. They assumed I'd just had the flu. No one suspected a thing when I returned, and frankly I was happy to have the distraction of work.

I kicked off my black heels as I entered the front door of my rather blandly decorated beach house that I was in the process of now livening up. Colorful paintings, red throw pillows on my white couch, and plants. Lots of big plants.

Bentley made his way from whichever place he'd been napping, greeting me with minimal enthusiasm.

I looked down at him and smiled. "I got some treats for you today. Wanna see?"

He stared with boredom until I whipped out a paper bag filled with crunchy gourmet chicken snaps.

"Want one?" I reached inside the bag, bent over, and held one to his nose so he could get a good whiff.

Bentley wagged his tail.

"That deserves a treat!" I handed it over. He

swallowed it in one gulp and then looked at me expectantly, wagging his short little spotted Jack Russell tail. "Okay. Just one more. But then I want to see more wagging and less attitude."

He gave me a little bark.

I handed over the treat and then scratched him behind the ear. "You like that, don't you, boy?" He pushed his nose into my hand and then rubbed his body on me. It turned out that what Bentley had been trying to tell me all along wasn't that he hated me, but that he was afraid. Whoever had been his owner before me wasn't nice to him. That was what I figured out the night I came home and cried, missing Mack (who was in Greece) and feeling so lost about the future. Bentley seemed nicer than a pillow, and I guess while I was holding him, I let out some of that light. From that moment on, he began to change. Some pain wasn't meant to be held onto forever.

"You got any of those tummy rubs for me?" said a deep voice from the open front door I'd forgotten to close.

I looked up and nearly wet my navy work slacks. Short, stylishly mussed jet black hair, a manicured five o'clock shadow that matched the curtain of inky black lashes surrounding piercing, sky blue eyes. And then there was that finely tailored suit that hugged his tall, powerful frame and broad shoulders.

"King?"

He stepped inside and shut the door, straightening his cufflinks like my presence bored the hell out of him and he was thinking of ten other places he'd rather be.

"No," he said with that masculine timbre. "But did I fool you?"

"Mack?" I jerked upright and took a small step forward. That was when I saw the devilish little smile appear.

He winked.

"Ohmygod." I rushed forward and threw my arms around his neck, bathing his face in kisses, while standing on my tiptoes. "I missed you. I missed you. I missed you."

Wait. Why's he dressed like... I pulled back. "What's going on with the uh...new look?" Mack was a rough-around-the-edges type—leather jacket, jeans, and probably only wore a suit when forced.

"Just because King is gone doesn't mean the work has ended."

"Meaning?"

"Meaning that Mia spent the week helping me perfect my King impersonation, which wasn't easy for her, but she knows how important it is. For all of us," he added.

I cringed. "Why?"

"Because the 10 Club still has to be dealt with and that has to be an inside job."

"So you're going to pose as your brother." That sounded extremely dangerous.

He nodded. "But I need you to help me with the icing."

"Okaaaay."

He pulled me tightly against him, and I could

smell his delicious, citrusy cologne mixed with the subtle natural musk of his skin and hair.

He smells like a sexy badass.

He continued, "And since the 10 Club members believe you're King's plaything, well, I thought you could help me perfect that part of my image, too."

My stomach began to fill with dangerous, hot little sparks. "You have no idea what you do to me."

"Why don't you tell me?" He moved a warm hand to the back of my neck.

"Looking at you, seeing you alive makes every inch of my body ache. In a good way." That was pretty weak compared to how I truly felt.

"Then why did you try to forget me?" There was a flicker of hurt in his eyes.

I could only offer him my best guess. "I think I lost hope."

"Whatever the reason, it's time to move forward." He released me, took my hand, and tugged me into the living room, pushing me to sit on my white sofa. He then kneeled his large, well-built frame in front of me.

"Do it. Take it away," he said.

It took me a moment to realize what he was asking. He finally wanted me to heal him, and for me, there was simply nothing in this world I wanted more. Than him, of course.

I studied Mack's new face. It was fucking beautiful. No. Beautiful was the wrong word. Beautiful was a flower or a sunset. His face was exquisite and masculine, and I still couldn't fully believe all this was real.

But it is...

"Okay. Here goes." From this moment on, he and I would be starting our life together. Not completely free of the past, but we'd be together and...well...uncursed. Hey, that was pretty nice.

I placed my hands on either side of his neck, beginning to focus on that little warm light.

"Wait. I'm not going to forget you, am I?" he asked.

I gave it a moment of thought. That light seemed to have a will all its own when it came to determining what a person needed, but I'd helped King lighten the load of his torment, and he turned out fine—more or less.

"I think we just have to see what will happen," I said. "But don't worry. If you forget me, I'll remind you." I leaned forward, threading my hand into his thick, soft, dark hair, and kissed him. Our lips melded, our tongues mingled, and I didn't know about him, but my heart began to accelerate. And somewhere in the back of my mind, it all felt familiar. Perhaps it was a vague memory of our first kiss over three thousand years ago in that small smoky hut somewhere in the jungle when he'd been a stranger from another land and captured my heart, when I had been willing to leave everything behind and risk my life just for the chance to be with him. I still felt the same.

It didn't take long for our kiss, with him still kneeling in front of the couch and me pulling him closer between my legs, to turn into a frenzy of want and need. He'd left me several weeks ago after

I thought I'd lost him forever, and I'd been waiting not-so-patiently to release my bottled-up tension.

I broke the kiss and quickly slid off his tie, unbuttoned his shirt, and then helped him shrug it off along with his blazer. His well-defined chest and arms and rippling abs were too incredible for words, except for... "Wow. I think I like this body even better."

He flashed a charming smile that produced little divots in his stubbly cheeks that instantly got me thinking about one thing and one thing only.

I stood up and pulled my white knit work blouse over my head and then quickly wiggled out of my slacks and underwear.

Still kneeling, Mack gazed up at me with those hungry eyes. "Once again, if I'd only known that showing you my manly abs would get me into your pants this fast, I would've led with that."

I chuckled and sat back down on the couch, pulling him between my thighs. He frantically unbuckled his belt and freed his hard cock. I glanced down at the thing, remembering how it looked when he first appeared at the burial site in his birthday suit. It had gotten much bigger.

"Geez. Is that larger than your last body?"

He shrugged proudly and then gripped my hips and slid me forward, a wolfish grin on his face.

Ohgod. I needed him so badly. He had no idea. Or maybe he did, because he went straight to giving me what I wanted: That large cock inside me.

He took his hard flesh in his hand and watched himself slowly entering, inch by inch, inside me, coaxing a soft moan from my mouth. He felt so incredible—the way he filled me so completely, the way he took pleasure in watching his shaft slide inside and connect our bodies, the way he looked at me with those eyes.

Once inside completely, he pressed his hands on the crease of my thighs and then pulled out again, ever so slowly. This was a slow kind of blissful torture, erotic as hell.

I moaned again as he repeated the act, savoring the slow burn of our bodies touching so intimately.

"No more, please. You're going to drive me mad."

"You want me to stop?"

"No, I meant—" I leaned forward and pulled him into me, kissing him hard. His sweet, sweet taste and smell only amplified my excitement.

He let loose and began pumping hard, our hips colliding, the pressure building. I then remembered what he'd asked of me, and without my even thinking about it, that light began to flow through my body into Mack as we made hard, hot love.

His mouth trailed down the side of my neck, kissing and licking everything in reach, while his strong hands cupped my breasts and his hips thrusted into me at the perfect pace, building the sweet tension pooling deep inside my core.

I didn't know if he was lost in the moment, in the sensation of our bodies moving together, pushing each other toward what we both knew would be a mind-blowing climax, but I don't think he realized what I was doing to the other part of him: his soul.

As I gripped his shoulders, feeling myself fall over that delicious edge, the light flowing through us, all I could think of was that it had all been worth it. For this moment of happiness, I would live it all over again.

The orgasm crashed through me without mercy, drawing a deep moan from my lips that pushed Mack over the edge. He arched his back and thrust one final time, coming hard. My body still flying somewhere up in the clouds, I heard Mack groan again in such a sensual tone, he sparked another round of delicious contractions.

He slowly pushed into me, still twitching as his cum continued to jet out, prolonging the moment for me.

Sooo...good... was all that came to mind.

After a few minutes, holding each other, sweaty and panting, Mack whispered in my ear, "I hope one of them gets lucky."

It took a moment for that to sink in.

"You mean your sperm?" I glanced at him sideways.

He made a little shrug and smiled before planting a lingering kiss on my collarbone. "I've been waiting a very long time to start my life. And so have you."

He was so right. "I hope one of them gets lucky, too."

Chapter Twenty-Four

After Mack and I had our hotter-than-hell reunion quickie on the sofa, we somehow made it to my bedroom and continued going at it for the next few hours—with a few breaks here and there for his new "equipment," of course. Mack licked and explored every inch of my body, and I reciprocated. His abs alone received a solid forty-five minutes of adoring kisses and affection.

All the while, I kept gloating over how great of a job I'd done healing him. That man was seriously happy. Glowing, radiant, sexy as hell, a fucking stallion of pleasure in bed, and utterly joyous. And he was totally focused one hundred percent on me. Not on curses. Not on skeletons in the closet. Just me.

Both of us lying down, gazing up at my white ceiling in a post-coital fog, I could honestly say it was the first time I recalled not thinking about anything. Not a damned thing. I was a giant ball of squishy, gooey, blissful emotions.

I sighed contentedly. "God, I'm so happy."

Mack chuckled. "I'm glad, because I feel obligated to make an honest woman out of you, and no one wants to be married to a grump."

I turned my head. He was smiling but still staring up at the ceiling.

"Married, huh? I dunnoooo. You're kinda old," I said.

He whipped his gaze my way. "I'm deeply offended. And I intend to punish you for that until you say yes."

I lifted a brow. "Promise?"

"Just as soon as I get us a glass of water." He slid from the bed, buck naked, giving me a genuinely stunning view of his perfect, hard, round ass and that powerful back and broad shoulders and…

God, that's so unfair. He's way too beautiful.

"Want anything?" he called out from the hallway as he made his way to my kitchen.

"Just you!"

I sighed and wiggled my toes underneath the sheets, beginning to mentally plan our wedding. First, we would take a long trip somewhere secluded and warm; then we'd marry—it would have to be an elopement—no, something chic and modest so my parents would be happy—and then we'd take another few week's honeymoon on some other gorgeous island. As for my job, well…I'd have to work something out with them, if they'd let me. I didn't want to run a center, I'd realized somewhere along this journey; I wanted to heal people and use my gift.

I wonder what Mack wants to do. Honestly, I had no idea what was involved in dismantling that 10 Club. I couldn't believe it would be easy or without some risk.

I seriously needed to ask him about that. Because on one hand, such a powerful group of degenerates could not be allowed to continue doing what they were doing. On the other hand, I wanted Mack safe and all to myself.

"A wise choice," said that deep, deep voice from the doorway.

I looked up at Mack, who now had his suit back on along with a very serious look on his face.

"Why did you get dressed?" I asked.

He stared at me without the slightest hint of kindness or affection in his eyes. That was when I noticed the ribbons of black swirling all around him.

What the...?

He continued staring with that hard, empty gaze, turning the room a frigid temperature that left my breath steaming in front of my face.

"The 10 Club stays," he said. "And tell my brother to stay *the fuck* out of my way."

I blinked, and he was gone. Poof!

Shivering like mad, I swallowed the lump of cold dread stuck in my throat.

"Hey! Your dog just tried to lick my d—Teddi? What's wrong?"

I looked at Mack, who stood in the doorway, buck naked, holding a tall glass of water in each hand.

I couldn't speak.

"Teddi? What the fuck is wrong?" Mack repeated.

Once again, I swallowed hard. "Umm..." I pointed my shaking hand at the doorway where the real Mack now stood. "Y-y-your br-br-brother."

"What about him?"

"He's back. And it's not the-the good one." It wasn't the living one either.

The glasses in Mack's hands slipped and crashed on the floor. "Fuck."

THE END?

(Okay...not the end.)

**Read on for more info about
the next book in the series!**

Author's Note

Hi, All!

Now, before anyone moans and says, "Uuuugh…another Mimi cliffhanger!" let me just defend myself by pointing out that it's technically a teaser for the next book since Mack did find his special someone and we finally got to find out what he'd been up to all those years.

BUT…is his journey over? Heck no! Neither is King's, Mia's, or Teddi's. Because there's still one more big piece of story missing to close out the original King Trilogy! So keep your eyes open for…

THE TEN CLUB

"I am the man who will kill anyone that gets in my way. And, Mack, you're in my fucking way." – King

Coming Fall 2016
For more book info:
www.mimijean.net/tenclub.html

And don't miss the upcoming cover reveal. (Yes! With a full-faced sexy, evil King!) Sign up for my mailing list: http://bit.ly/1MBt4HR

I don't know about you, but I'm excited to see Mack and King face off! (I wonder if they could solve their issues with a nude mud-wrestling match. Hmm…)

Anyway, moving on…I know posting reviews can be a serious pain in the butt, but I am FOREVER grateful when you do them. YES! They still matter. So please DO remember to mention when you post one and request MACK SWAG (mimi@mimijean.net). I'll be sure to throw in some extra goodies! (Likely, I'll have Tommaso and God of Wine swag soon! Yum.)

AND! For you folks who enjoy the book breakdowns, I added one for you after the playlist below!

Okay then, off you go! Find happy, tasty book treats and report back to the rest of us.

Happy Reading,
Mimi

P.S. Want to hear what was playing while I wrote this book?

MACK PLAYLIST:

"Trouble" by Ray LaMontagne

"10,000 Emerald Pools" by Børns

"Dug My Heart" by Børns

"Past Lives" by Børns

"Electric Love" by Børns

"Tear In My Heart" by Twenty One Pilots

"Forgive & Forget" by The Kooks

"Thank God for Girls" by Weezer

"Sweet Disposition" by The Temper Trap

"You Are The Best Thing" by Ray LaMontagne

"Ain't No Sunshine" by Bill Withers

"Holy Ghost" by Børns

"Space Oddity" by David Bowie (RIP, you awesome man.)

"Ride" by Twenty One Pilots

"Alive" by Sia

"Back To Black" by Amy Winehouse

WHAT'S MACK REALLY ALL ABOUT?

Okay, so this story's meaning isn't as complex as some of the others I write, but it's a theme I'm sure we can all relate to. Ready? It's about love! I know...shocker, right? LOL. But in this case, it's about the love we need versus the love we're given.

I'm sure some of you are thinking, "Mimi, don't get all squirrelly and philosophical on us!" But I fear I must! Haha…

Because now that I have two growing boys, who always seem at odds with my definition of love, it's a topic front and center in my life. They always want. I always want to give. But I know in the back of my mind that if I really love them, I'll give them what they need (but it won't make them happy). This has really made me start to think about the true definition of love: making someone I love happy, which makes me happy, versus making their lives better.

Okay, so the parent-child analogy is easy. But when you migrate into the grown-up world, the lines begin to blur.

We've all been guilty of doing something in the name of love, only to discover that the recipient (sibling, spouse, friend, etc.) of our sacrifice wasn't so pleased. Or we've been on the receiving end of the "gift" of love that wasn't what we needed. The point is that many times people THINK they're helping and giving love when in reality our true needs never crossed their minds.

King kept killing off Teddi, thinking he was saving his brother from dying. When, in reality, he was destroying this person he loved. Because what Mack really needed was King to just be his brother and show him compassion. Like himself, Mack had lived through hell and was struggling with his own demons. But because Mack was the "suffer in silence" type, he never asked King for what he really needed—he didn't really know how. And King just kept on giving and giving (death to poor Teddi).

Likewise, King had asked Mack to end his life (in Minoa). King used the excuse of love ("if you love me, you'll do this" argument), but the truth was that what King really needed was for his brother to give him a kick in the pants. They were both too blind to see it.

The point is that love isn't always giving the other person what they want. Love isn't always giving them what *you* want. Love is about making those hard choices and laddering up to see the big picture so you can give the other person what they truly need. But that, too, is what it's all about: taking the time to think it through and honor your special relationship by giving it the attention it's worth. I need to do more of this in my life, for sure!

I know this didn't blow anyone's mind, but that's what the story is about (and is a reflection of what's been going on in my life).

So! I hope you enjoyed, because the next chapter of the King Series is going to be frivolously gluttonous, hot alpha-man-archy! (Hey, it's no fun to be deep all the time! LOL.)
HAPPY READING,
Mimi

Acknowledgements

First, a huge thank you to Dali for all of her incredible support these past months and for catching the fact that I left out the most important part of the book: saying THANK YOU! (Yep. It's true. I totally missed it.) I've been way over my head lately, so it's great to have people I can count on and keep the wheels on the Mimi Bus! So, as always, I give my undying gratitude to not just Dali, but Kylie Gilmore, Latoya Smith, Pauline Nolet, and Stef. I can't forget Ally and Bridget, too! Thank you for always pitching in.

As always, my family gets the lion's share of my gratitude for being there to support me day in and day out.

Finally, THERE ARE MY AWESOME READERS and TEAM MINKY. THANK YOU for continuing to believe in me. You make it all possible.

Mimi

Tommaso

Immortal Matchmakers, Inc. Book #2
COMING MAY 2016

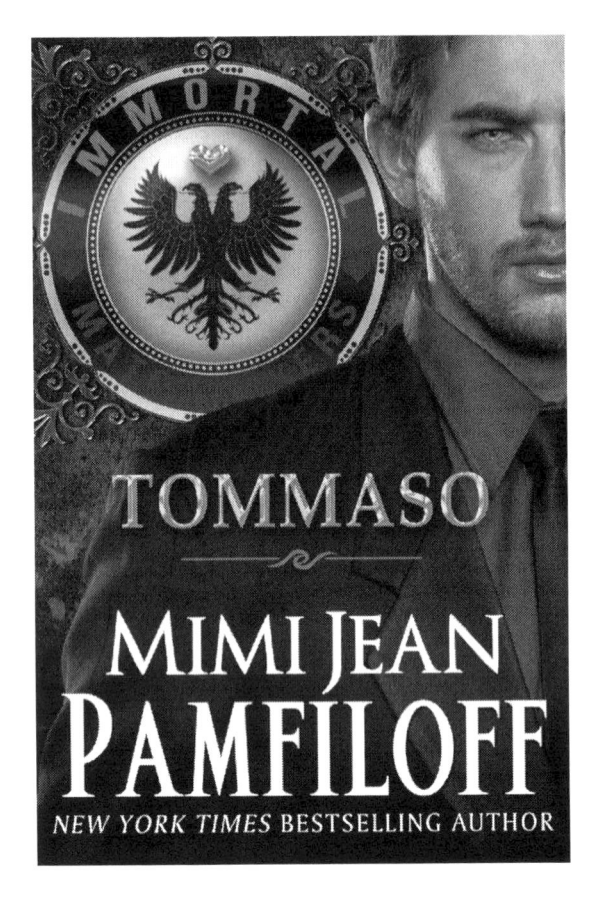

FOR BOOK EXTRAS, BUY LINKS, and NEWS:
www.mimijean.net/immortal_matchmakers.html

GOD OF WINE

Immortal Matchmakers, Inc. Book #3
COMING 2016

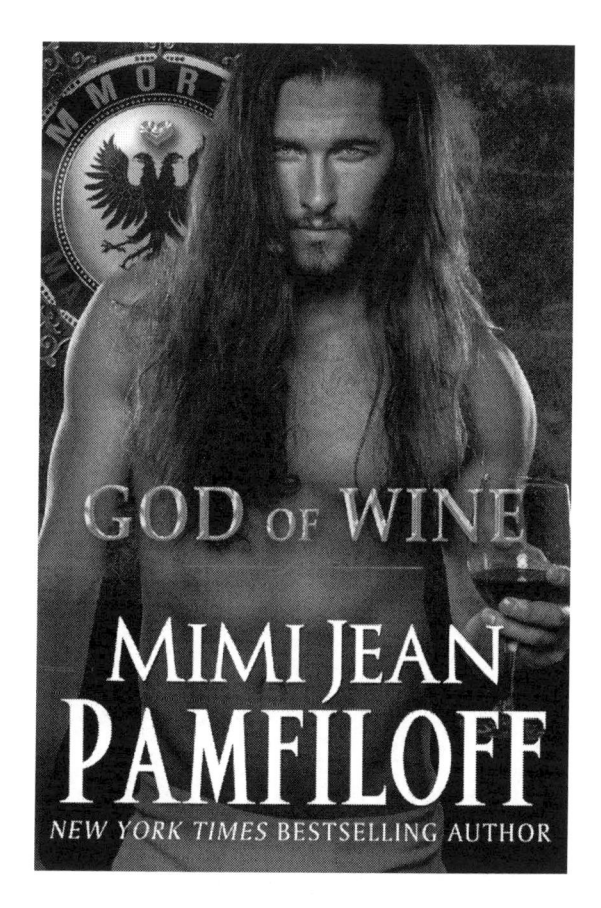

FOR BUY LINKS, BOOK EXTRAS, AND NEWS:
www.mimijean.net/immortal_matchmakers.html

The Happy Pants Series is Back!

TAILORED FOR TROUBLE
Coming August 2016

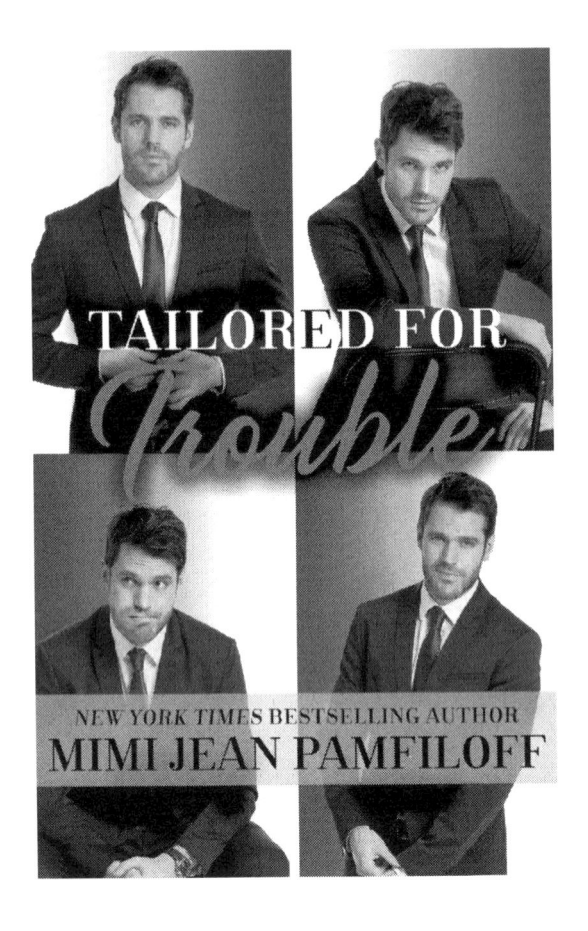

Yeah, I know…It took me awhile, but Happy Pants is back! And this book...THIS BOOK!...is so special to me. It's the full Mimi buffet—funny, crazy, sexy, twisty, and deep. I love this book with all my heart, and I hope you do, too.

FOR BUY LINKS, EXCERPTS, and MORE:
www.mimijean.net/tailored.html

About the Author

Mimi Jean Pamfiloff is a *New York Times* & *USA Today* best-selling author of Paranormal and Contemporary Romance. Her books have been #1 genre sellers around the world. Both traditionally and independently published, Mimi has sold over 700,000 books since publishing her first title in 2012, and she plans to spontaneously combust once she hits the one million mark. Although she obtained her international MBA and worked for over 15 years in the corporate world, she believes that it's never too late to come out of the romance closet and follow your dream.

When not screaming at her computer, Mimi spends time with her two pirates in training, her loco-for-the-chili-pepper hubby, and her rat terriers, Mini and DJ Princess Snowflake, in the San Francisco Bay Area.

She continues to hope that her books will inspire a leather pants comeback (for men) and that she might make you laugh when you need it most.

Sign up for Mimi's giveaways and new release news!

http://bit.ly/1MBt4HR

LEARN MORE:

www.mimijean.net

twitter.com/MimiJeanRomance

www.facebook.com/MimiJeanPamfiloff

Made in the USA
Charleston, SC
12 February 2016